DARTMOOR
NATIONAL PARK

Edited by
John Weir

Webb&Bower
MICHAEL JOSEPH

Acknowledgements
All the photographs in this book were taken for the
Countryside Commission by Chris Chapman and Brian
Pearce.

Based on an original text by Mark Beeson

First published in Great Britain 1987 by
Webb & Bower (Publishers) Limited
9 Colleton Crescent, Exeter, Devon EX2 4BY
in association with Michael Joseph Limited
27 Wright's Lane, London W8 5SL
and The Countryside Commission,
John Dower House, Crescent Place,
Cheltenham, Glos GL50 3RA

Designed by Ron Pickless

Production by Nick Facer/Rob Kendrew

Illustrations by Rosamund Gendle/Ralph Stobart

Text and new photographs Copyright © The Countryside Commission
Illustrations Copyright © Webb & Bower (Publishers) Ltd

British Library Cataloguing in Publication Data
The National parks of Britain.
Dartmoor
1. National parks and reserves — England —
Guide-books 2. England — Description and
travel — 1971– — Guide-books.
I. Beeson, Mark
914.2′04858 SB484.G7.

ISBN 0-86350-139-7

Typeset in Great Britain by Keyspools Ltd., Golborne, Lancs.

Printed and bound in Hong Kong by Mandarin Offset.

Contents

Preface

Dartmoor is one of ten national parks which were established in the 1950s. These largely upland and coastal areas represent the finest landscapes in England and Wales and present us all with opportunities to savour breathtaking scenery, to take part in invigorating outdoor activities, to experience rural community life, and most certainly, to relax in peaceful surroundings.

The designation of national parks is the product of those who had the vision, more than fifty years ago, to see that ways were found to ensure that the best of our countryside should be recognized and protected, the way of life therein sustained, and public access for open-air recreation encouraged.

As the government planned Britain's post-war reconstruction, John Dower, architect, rambler and national park enthusiast, was asked to report on how the national park ideal adopted in other countries could work for England and Wales. An important consideration was the ownership of land within the parks. Unlike other countries where large tracts of land are in public ownership, here in Britain most of the land within the national parks was, and still is, privately owned. John Dower's report was published in 1945 and its recommendations accepted. Two years later another report drafted by a committee chaired by Sir Arthur Hobhouse proposed an administrative system for the parks, and this was embodied in the National Parks and Access to the Countryside Act 1949.

This Act set up the National Parks Commission to designate national parks and advise on their administration. In 1968 this became the Countryside Commission but we continue to have national responsibility for our parks which are administered by local government, either through committees of the county councils or independent planning boards.

This guide to the landscape, settlements and natural history of Dartmoor National Park is one of a series on all ten parks. As well as helping the visitor appreciate the park and its attractions, the guides outline the achievements and pressures facing the national park authorities today.

Our national parks are a vital asset, and we all have a duty to care for and conserve them. Learning about the parks and their value to us all is a crucial step in creating more awareness of the importance of the national parks so that each of us can play our part in seeing that they are protected for all to enjoy.

Sir Derek Barber, Chairman, Countryside Commission

Introduction

Dartmoor is situated in the southern part of the county of Devon, and is the most southerly national park in Britain, covering an area of 365 square miles. Its core consists of a high, rolling upland, which might best be described as having three distinct sections: the North Moor, where the highest ground is, the South Moor, and the East Moor, each section being more or less divided from the others by the branches of the River Dart. The North and South Moors are predominantly peat-covered plateaux with low relief, but on the East Moor relief is more pronounced. The North Moor rises to a height of 2,039 ft (619 m) at High Willhays, which is the highest point in England south of the Peak District. Though the outline of the central hills is essentially smooth, it is broken in places by the jagged outcrops of tors, especially on the East Moor and nearer the fringes. Here rivers run through 'cleaves' and gorges, and the hills lift steeply from the surrounding country.

The climate is wet, but not as cold as that of other British uplands further north. The average annual rainfall is 60 in (144 mm), but this varies considerably from place to place, the wetter western side sometimes receiving over 100 in (240 mm). The prevailing wind is south westerly, and may reach gale force on summits.

In spite of the Moor's proximity to the south coast, its elevation means that snow is common in winter. Villages and farms are frequently cut off for short periods by blizzards. In summer, on the other hand, it is not unheard of for people walking on fine days to suffer from heat exhaustion.

Dartmoor's relatively undisturbed open moorland contains plant communities that are of particular interest for their combination of northern and southern elements. It also provides a good breeding habitat for a number of species of upland birds, some of them at the southern limit of their range. In the steep river valleys around the edge of the upland, broad-leaved woods play a significant part in the appearance and ecology of the landscape, providing a refuge for the more

Greator Rocks reveal Dartmoor's granite face.

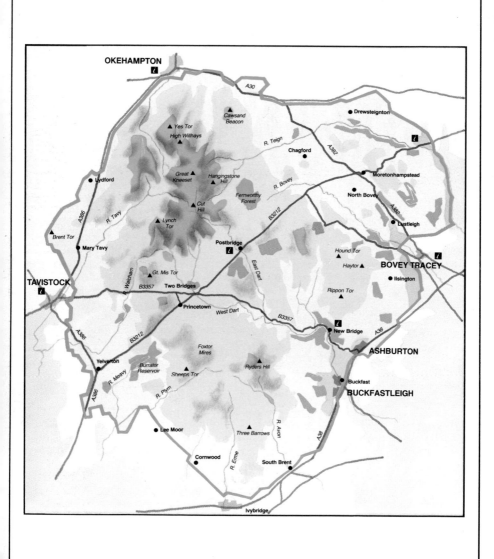

Waterfall, East Dart River. The River Dart is one of twelve main rivers that rise on Dartmoor and is so called from the swiftness of its current. Twin sources initiate the lengthy branches of the West and East Dart Rivers which ultimately unite at Dartmeet. Often described as the loveliest river in England, the river is fed by fifty-five distinct tributaries.

Facing The Dartmoor National Park.

secretive mammals. Dartmoor is the only national park where the area of broad-leaved woodland exceeds that of coniferous plantations.

Dartmoor is also home to people. A landscape of prehistoric remains hardly paralleled in Europe bears witness to a long tradition of upland settlement. At the time of the 1981 census, 30,000 people were living within the national park boundary. Ashburton is the largest town, with a population of around 3,500. Of the 10,900 people in employment, the majority were in service industries (including transport) and in manufacturing, with only thirteen per cent in agriculture. The number of farm holdings declined from 2,388 in 1952 to 1,612 in 1975, but agriculture remains the characteristic activity of the district, eighty-seven per cent of the total area being farmed. Some 94,000 acres, representing forty per cent of the national park, are registered as common land, with an ancient tradition of use by the people of the moorland parishes and other parts of the county.

Dartmoor's relatively large area of unenclosed moorland and its valley broad-leaved woodland, combined with its imposing array of prehistoric remains and its integrity as uninterrupted upland, made it a candidate for designation as a national park when the national park movement gained

A typical Dartmoor scene where moorland and valley farmland meet. Here is a diversity of relief and vegetation with a unity involving a pleasing and balanced inter-relationship between nature and the efforts of man.

strength in the 1930s. Pioneers of the modern appreciation of Dartmoor such as Robert Burnard and Hansford Worth, both members of the Dartmoor Exploration Committee which began the scientific investigation of Dartmoor's archaeological wealth, had been talking about some sort of park since the closing decades of the nineteenth century. In 1937 the Dartmoor Preservation Association declared that Dartmoor's best interests would be served by creating a national park. Designation finally came in 1951, following the 1949 National Parks and Access to the Countryside Act.

Dartmoor's character is not one of 'wilderness' in the modern sense of the word, as used for instance of the American national parks. It is an expanse which even in its remotest parts is managed by humans and bears their stamp over thousands of years.

The startling juxtaposition of barren and rich, of human and elemental, is also reflected in Dartmoor's tin-mining past, the remains of which are as ubiquitous as those of prehistoric settlement. This allies the area closely with the granite regions of Cornwall, to which it is geologically related, Dartmoor being in geological terms something of a Cornish outcrop in England. The Dartmoor we value today subtly reflects the integration of the whole spectrum of human economic activity, from industry to farming, with history, landscape and wildlife. If Dartmoor can stand as model for this, it may serve as inspiration for the conservation or indeed the renovation of many areas of countryside and wasteland far less well championed but of great importance to the people who live near or in them.

1 The birth and legacy of the area

A separated rock pile, Houndtor, with Haytor in the distance. Here granite has been exposed as a jagged series of blocks divided and grooved into shelves, pillars, battlements and buttresses by the action of weathering on the joints and bedding planes in the rock.

Permanence is one of the strongest impressions conveyed by the rocks of Dartmoor as they stand today. But in geological terms the granite is not particularly old and the tors in their present form are very new. Wandering across Leusdon Common, where the rock changes from granite to hornfels, or staring at the fantastic shapes of Houndtor, it is of course possible to appreciate both characteristics as variations in the landscape without enquiring further. But any attempt to understand why people have used Dartmoor in the way they have, and what constraints there are on its present and future uses, must begin with a study of its origins. For in its origins lie the best clues to Dartmoor's intrinsic potential and limitations. Neither the granite nor the tors have always been there, and like all things that

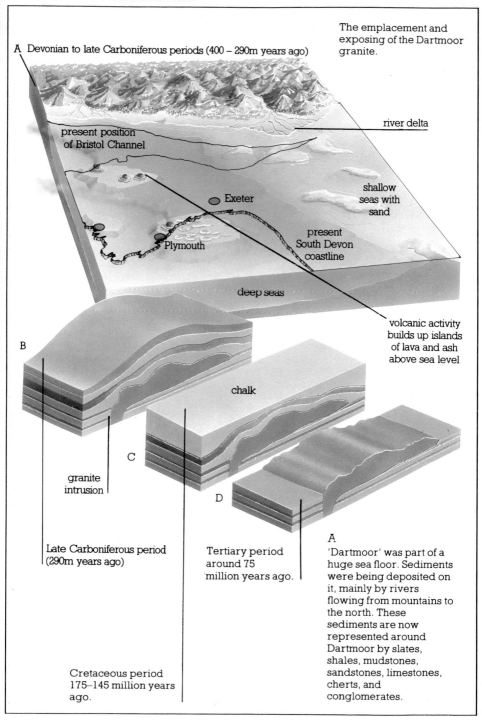

The emplacement and exposing of the Dartmoor granite.

A Devonian to late Carboniferous periods (400 – 290m years ago)

river delta

present position of Bristol Channel

Exeter

shallow seas with sand

Plymouth

present South Devon coastline

deep seas

volcanic activity builds up islands of lava and ash above sea level

B

chalk

C

granite intrusion

D

Late Carboniferous period (290m years ago)

Tertiary period around 75 million years ago.

A

'Dartmoor' was part of a huge sea floor. Sediments were being deposited on it, mainly by rivers flowing from mountains to the north. These sediments are now represented around Dartmoor by slates, shales, mudstones, sandstones, limestones, cherts, and conglomerates.

Cretaceous period 175–145 million years ago.

are born, they are in the process of ageing, and therefore changing. Likewise Dartmoor in its various geological aspects has had many different living inhabitants, and it is worth considering their comings and goings in order to appreciate just how brief our own human occupation has been and how precarious its future may be.

Some 400 million years ago, when the earliest rocks still evident in Devon were formed, the area we now know as 'Dartmoor' was part of a huge sea floor. From early Devonian until late Carboniferous times (400–290 million years ago), sediments were being constantly deposited on it, mainly carried down by rivers from mountains to its north. Around Dartmoor these sediments are now represented by slates, shales, mudstones, sandstones, cherts, limestones and conglomerates, and the younger, Carboniferous deposits in this sequence are known here as 'Culm Measures'. Meanwhile, sporadic volcanic eruptions on the sea floor produced local areas of volcanic rocks, such as ashes and lavas. The fossil-bearing limestones of Ashburton and Buckfastleigh, and those close to Okehampton, derived as they are from corals and other marine invertebrates, indicate that life-forms were already beginning to play a part in forming the landscape whose surface has come to be dominated by living influences, notably man.

On the land to the north and south of this sea, the first forest, with palm- and fern-like trees such as can still be seen in parts of Africa, were colonized by arthropods, including insects, and later by

B
During the late Carboniferous period the sedimentary rocks were subject to intense pressure from the north and south resulting in their crumpling into a folded mountain chain known as the Cornubian Mountains. Beneath these folds magma welled up into the rocks of the new mountains. The Magma cooled to form granite.

C
The Cornubian Mountains had been eroded away during the Permian and Triassic periods and Dartmoor was again submerged under a shallow sea and a thin layer of chalk deposited on it.

D
Soft chalk had been eroded away. Earth movements in the late Cretaceous and mid Tertiary period gave Dartmoor its present-day outline as new river courses and agents of weathering attacked the granite.

amphibians. But the space that is now Dartmoor was home to marine plant and animal communities, among them the earliest bony fishes.

About 290 million years ago, at the end of this deposition, movements in the Earth's crust, which were part of a great mountain building period, folded the sediments of Devon along an east–west axis, producing what geologists know as the Cornubian Mountains. Into the roots of these mountains was intruded a mass of molten granite now lying across the South West from the Scilly Isles to Dartmoor, in a series of 'bosses', which are all linked within the crust, and of which Dartmoor is the largest. The Dartmoor intrusion rose from the depth in the south and spread northward where the base of the granite may only be at a depth of three to four miles. As the hot granite was thrust into the surrounding host rocks, it distorted and baked them. These altered rocks now form a zone around Dartmoor known as the 'metamorphic aureole' in which, for instance, sandstones have become hornfels and limestones changed to marbles.

The granite itself is composed of four principal minerals: the glistening flakes of mica (usually biotite which is browny-black, or, occasionally, muscovite, which is white), the two felspars (white orthoclase and grey plagioclase), which sometimes appear as very dominant large rectangular crystals in most tors, and glass-like quartz. These minerals are weathered at different rates by surface water. The first to be affected is biotite, whose decay by oxidization leaves a reddish-brown staining, often to be seen around the edge of boulders in the ground. The felspars are subject to breakdown into kaolin, or china clay, well seen at Lee Moor in south-west

Metamorphic rock on Leusdon Common. Dartmoor's granite mass is surrounded by sedimentary rocks greatly altered by the heat and pressure caused by its intrusion some 290 million years ago.

Merrivale the only working granite quarry surviving today. Durability, strength and abundance has meant that, until recently, granite has hardly ever taken second place to any other stone for building use on Dartmoor proper since prehistoric times.

Dartmoor. This leaves quartz, the mineral most resistant to chemical weathering. It remains in the rotted granite, or 'growan' as it is called locally, with the cores of rotten felspars, in the form of gravel until, with leaching, the quartz may form as much as ninety per cent of the gravel. Despite its chemical vulnerability, sound granite is physically strong and makes a very durable building material, which is thus difficult to handle, and to work.

The appearance of the granite from different parts of the Moor, and even within single outcrops, is by no means uniform. There are three basic types: a dark granite with fragments of altered sedimentary rocks where the old host rock fell into the hot igneous intruder; a coarse granite distinguished by the frequency of its large felspar crystals (the so-called 'tor' or 'giant' granite), and a fine-grained 'aplogranite' which lacks the large felspar crystals. The so-called 'blue' granite, to be seen for instance in the lower western part of Haytor Rocks, represents the contact face of a separate later intrusion into the granite. It is in fact aplogranite, which occurs within the tor granite in veins. There is a good example at Corndon Tor, where tor granite above is separated from tor granite below by a narrow band of aplogranite. The current view is that the tor granite represents a near-contact face of the igneous intrusion with the surrounding sedimentary rocks. The grain of Dartmoor granite generally becomes finer the further down from the surface it is quarried (a fact which saved the tors from being dismantled by the industrial quarrymen of the . nineteenth century, since they valued the finer grain more highly).

As the granite cooled it was altered in places by gases and vapours. This process is called 'pneumatolysis'. For example, black biotite was replaced with white muscovite, or in other cases by tourmaline, blacker than biotite and distinguishable by its finely grooved surface. Kaolinization on the grand scale is also a result of pneumatolysis in some areas of the South West around Lee Moor where china clay is worked today, though in most other places in Dartmoor kaolinization is a surface phenomenon produced by chemical weathering.

Pneumatolysis was also responsible for metalliferous minerals. Dartmoor was less well endowed with metals than the Cornish granite, but tin ore (cassiterite) occurred in abundance, often associated with copper, arsenic, lead, zinc, silver, iron and wolfram or tungsten. These minerals tended to be laid down in concentric zones, with tin, which solidified nearest the still hot granite, at the centre. Major emanative centres occurred at Birch

Spoil from a long abandoned tin mine showing cassiterite (tin ore).

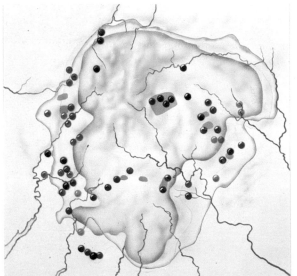

National park boundary

Granite

Metamorphic aureole

Known emanative centre

Tin

Copper

Lead

Iron

Wolfram

Dartmoor Mining: main emanative centres

Tor, Mary Tavy and Holne Moor where the granite is impregnated by mineral veins. But alluvial tin covered valley floors over wide areas of Dartmoor at the end of the last Ice Age, deposited there by sludging and meltwater. There was a certain amount of gold with it, and gold can still be panned in minute quantities from Dartmoor streams. Copper lodes occur in the rocks of the metamorphic aureole, likewise lead and silver. The iron minerals, specular and micaceous haematite, occur in the Dartmoor tin lodes, while the magnetic iron ore, magnetite, has been mined near Haytor.

At the time of the granite intrusion, and well above it, what was to become Dartmoor stood exposed for the first time as the Cornubian Mountains. The semi-arid conditions with wind, temperature change and intermittent torrential rain that ensued in the Permian and Triassic periods (from 270 to 200 million years ago) induced severe weathering and erosion. So severe was this erosion that the granite mass was eventually attacked – we know the erosion reached so far down because of granitic particles in the St Cyres Beds just north of the Moor. The whole product of this erosion was carried down to form some of the New Red Sandstone, including clays, breccias, conglomerates and marls, which are visible from Dartmoor in the ploughed fields of the richest parts of lowland Devon, for instance around Crediton and alongside the Teign Estuary. Through this dusty landscape moved reptiles including the first dinosaurs. Such trees as there were are likely to have been giant conifers.

As the climate became milder during the following Jurassic period, forests of ginkgos, conifers and cycads dominated the vegetation almost everywhere on land, and Dartmoor would have had its share of the larger dinosaurs which thrived in this environment.

After the deposition of the New Red Sandstone, a gap in the record of the rocks occurs in west Devon, but we know from elsewhere that during the Cretaceous period (145–75 million years ago) Dartmoor was again submerged under a shallow sea and a thin layer of chalk was deposited on it. The chalk platform that covered much of Britain was then lifted and tilted slightly eastwards. The plateau area of Dartmoor as we know it today was finally in place, though it did not yet stand out from the surrounding land.

The sea retreated (at the start of the Tertiary

period, some seventy-five million years ago), and eastward-flowing rivers went to work on the soft chalk, carving out courses which are the ancestors of the upper reaches of modern rivers such as the Teign and Dart. Down below, the old eastward-flowing course of the rivers established as a result of the slope may still be represented east of Ashburton and along the Teign Estuary. Granite pebbles from Dartmoor have been found in the gravels of Haldon Hill, immediately to the east of the Moor, and as far away as Poole Harbour, deposited there by these Tertiary rivers.

The change from this eastward regional slope to the southward one we see today in the predominantly southward-flowing drainage pattern of south Devon, was the result of more crustal movements, the same ones which produced the Alps. In Devon they also caused tear-faults, the most important group of which runs from Torbay to Barnstaple, and is known as the Sticklepath Fault. The village of Sticklepath on the north-east edge of Dartmoor stands right on the main crack, and in 1955 was actually shaken by a tremor. The parallel valleys of the Bovey and the Wray Rivers and the Tottiford and Kennick Reservoirs are all associated

The River Erme, southern Dartmoor. The elevation of Dartmoor's southern plateau had been equal to that of the north until the tilting of the land left the highest parts in the north west, at High Willhays. This initiated the flow and valley excavation of the south-flowing rivers we see today.

The River Erme is here flanked by Piles Copse – one of three remaining relict broad-leaf woods on high Dartmoor.

Tor formation: By Tertiary times (about 75 million years ago) granite lay exposed as overlying sedimentary deposits had been eroded away. Chemical and mechanical weathering attacked the domed granite outcrops rising above tropical evergreen and semi-evergreen forests. Arctic conditions during and immediately after the Pleistocene Ice Age (600,000–10,000 years ago) broke up exposed granite through constant freezing and thawing of water along the joints; fallen blocks form the 'clitter' around the bases of tors. Characteristic trees of European temperate forest – such as hazel, birch, oak and elm – spread quickly as the climate improved following the last glaciation phase. Seasonal freezing still continues to attack the tors.

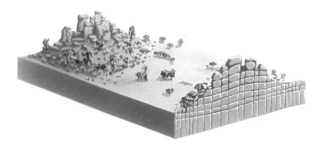

with this faulting, and between Bovey Tracey and Newton Abbot the resulting subsidence produced a large lake, into which a great thickness of sediments from the granite was carried and is still there as the gravels and clays around Bovey Tracey.

West of the faultline, the whole of the landscape was tilted southward. The present summits of Dartmoor decline progressively from the north west to south east, reflecting the combination of a tilt eastward and then southward, which is likewise reflected in the southerly trend in the headwaters of the Dart, the lower reaches of the Teign, the Bovey and the Dart, and also in the Erme, Avon and Harbourne.

The Tertiary climate was tropical, and did not produce the hot dusty conditions needed for accelerated erosion but it did allow enough to remove any last trace of chalk and other sediments, and renew the attack on the granite. The rise of mammals and flowering plants (including broad-leaved trees, and grasses) meant that Dartmoor's Tertiary ecosystem started to resemble more closely some of those that exist in other parts of the world today. The weather was generally moist and humid, and a flora with distinct tropical affinities covered much of Britain. We have a particularly good idea of the composition of the flora on Dartmoor from remains found in the Bovey Tracey lignite deposits. These are derived from plant material carried down into the lake with the sediments from the granite upland. About a third of the plant species represented in the deposits belong to genera which are now confined to the tropics.

Though there are only insects in the lignite at Bovey Tracey, the mammal fauna must have had similar tropical affinities. Evergreen and semi-evergreen forests grew below the domed outcrops of granite – forerunners of the tors – like those on the plateaux of present-day Eastern and Southern Africa. Since Dartmoor, unlike the uplands to the north, was never glaciated, its basic landscape pattern was more or less formed by the end of the Tertiary period, and in this surface sense, as opposed to the strictly geological, the landscape is very old, giving a rare continuity between then and the times in which the higher mammals and our ancestors evolved.

Part of the importance of considering the history of life forms on the Moor along with that of the evolving rocks lies in their contribution to the nutrient content of contemporary soils. The presence of tropical forest must have considerably slowed down weathering and erosion of the soil and the organic detritus of the monkeys and other fauna would also have more or less replaced the base minerals (particularly calcium) removed by leaching, hence preserving the pH balance of the soils.

Dartmoor's present outline is dominated by a series of level expanses or 'erosion surfaces' weathered and eroded during Tertiary times. The highest summits are assumed to be remnants of an original plain, lower on the southern plateau because of the mid-Tertiary tilt. The trough of the West Dart was cut into this surface and the remnants of successive floors of its wide shallow valley are evident in the spurs around Hexworthy and Sherberton. Below about 700 ft (212 m) at the edge of the Moor and usually off the granite, there is evidence for 'marine platforms' or ancient shorelines, created when Dartmoor was an island during the early Pleistocene (around two million years ago).

The erosion surfaces on the Moor, for instance, above the West Dart trough, south of Bellever Tor,

A moorland slope scattered with 'clitter' – the debris of a weathered and disintegrated tor.

are reminiscent of African land forms in the way that they are backed by short steep hillsides, and may have been similarly formed under tropical or sub-tropical conditions persisting into late Tertiary times.

Although never glaciated, Dartmoor was significantly affected by the action of deep, penetrating frost during the Pleistocene Ice Age (600,000–10,000 years ago). The whole process, together with the change in flora and fauna brought about by a cooler climate, resulted in the transition from an African-like to a distinctly northern European landscape. But a resemblance with parts of highland Africa still lingers in visual, geological, and perhaps also (as we shall see) ecological terms.

At their furthest extent on land, the glaciers and ice-sheets of the Ice Age reached the Bristol Channel. Devon was thus seasonally snow-covered but not glaciated during these ice-sheet advances, rather like Spitzbergen and northern Canada today. In the cold stages, frost action modified the landscape in two major ways: it began by filling in valleys and smoothing the slopes between them by moving soil and decomposed granite gradually downhill; then in a later stage it broke up the exposed solid granite through constant freezing and thawing of water along the joints in the rock, leaving previously smooth domes in a craggy, gapped and ruinous state, and scattering the new slopes below them with the debris of granite blocks known as 'clitter'. The summits tended to lose most material wherever their vertical jointing was most frequent – for instance, at Haytor Rocks the tor is lowest where the joints are closest together. The many roadside pits on the Moor are good places to see evidence of

the downhill movement of frost-weathered material.
A gravelly 'head', covering most of Dartmoor with
its crystal and rock fragments derived from frost
shattering, reveals the spread of debris across
gentle slopes by the agitation and sludging induced
by continual freezing and thawing.

Just as hot conditions had created the basic
Dartmoor outline, so many of the details of the
present-day granite area were fashioned by cold,
which roughened the tors and clitter slopes, while
smoothing the valley floors and land away from the
steep slopes. On the metamorphosed sedimentary
and volcanic rocks of the aureole, 'benches' or
ledges are the result of different degrees in
shattering in exposed metamorphic rock faces. The
bench effects at Sourton Tors, Peek Hill and Cox Tor
contrast markedly with the smooth convex descent
of granite hills such as Hameldown and Cosdon
Beacon. During the thawing phases the rivers were
torrential and incised their valleys deeply to

Sourton Tors, north-west
Dartmoor, rise from three
dykes of igneous rock on
a base of altered slates
and shales. Here, as on
other edges of Dartmoor,
the slates and shales have
been selectively eroded
to form benched hill
slopes known as
'altiplanation surfaces'.

produce the steep-sided gorges of the Dart, Teign
and others. Such torrents left the jumbled boulder
deposits just visible at Ivybridge and Newbridge
and very obviously at Becka Falls.

All this geological history being told, it is still the
tors which strike the visitor to Dartmoor as most
singular. Tors owe their particular shapes to the
pattern of cracks, or joints, which they all exhibit.
Near-vertical ones were formed as the granite
originally cooled and contracted; some of the others
as that cooling penetrated inwards and caused
concentric cracking and thus a structure like that of
an onion; yet more as the load of sedimentary rock

Greator Rocks
(foreground), Holwell
quarry (middle distance),
and Haytor, on
Dartmoor's eastern
moorland block.

above was eroded away, and, relieved of the weight, the granite sprang apart. Finally, as granite itself was removed, so cracks developed sub-parallel with valley sides – well seen at Bench Tor on the south bank of the Dart near Holne.

As to location, some summits – especially near the edge of the granite (Haytor, Rippon Tor, Ugborough Beacon for instance) – may have been very close to the original roof of the granite. Most, nevertheless, must have been formed during that long tropical phase of the Tertiary era. The tors of Bellever, Sittaford, and Great Mis Tor are on such hilltops. There are yet others on spur-ends, like Combestone and Vixen, and more at the lip of the most recent valley-sides – Ger Tor above the Tavy, Bench Tor above the Dart and a myriad of small tors in most valleys.

There is no doubt that this combination of patterns of dense fractures – and most exposed locations – summits, spur-ends and valley slips – was bound to be easily exploited by all the weathering and erosive agencies available through time. Warm, tropical, slightly acid rain penetrated all cracks beneath the forest floor, and widened them by corroding the felspars and the mica. Once the joints were exposed yet more rain could sluice away the rotten gravel between the blocks still *in situ*. Tropical tors are doubtless developed this way. The smoother outline of some of Dartmoor lends credibility to this hypothesis for their origin. But we know that at least four arctic-type attacks have been made on each location since the last tropical period. Every exposed joint filled with water or blown snow. Then ice crystals grew, expanded and levered one block away from its neighbour. On finally falling, the summer porridge of mud and gravel on top of the permafrost accelerated the movement of the block downslope, to clog the valley floor or to be borne away in the next flood of meltwater. The rugged, jagged and castellated tors must owe their form to this particular process. What we see is the result of the last freezing, now frozen in time until the next.

Between the four cold spells which constitute the most recent Ice Age, the interglacials were warmer than today's climate. Oceanic heath, like that on the present north-west European coastline, probably characterized the beginning and end of each warm period with mixed coniferous and deciduous woodland in the middle. During these warm periods a strange mixture of southern and northern

animals was present. The interglacial fossil remains
in caves at Buckfastleigh – which seem to have been
natural traps for wandering animals in the limestone
floor of the proto-Dart valley – include animal
families once confined to the tropics, such as lion,
elephant, hyena and rhinoceros. In other caves in
the Dart valley system there are contemporary
remains of northern temperate species such as wolf,
bear and beaver. Into this fascinating mixture and its
complex and evolving habitat for the first time
came men who also, of course, had tropical origins.

We may be in an interglacial today – some 12,000
years in – and our vegetation has developed in that
time since the dying years of the last glaciation. At
first, arctic/alpine ground plants were quickly
followed by trees. Pollen analysis has shown that
one of the first colonizers was juniper, followed by
pine and dwarf birch with a shrub layer of dwarf
willow. As the climate improved, characteristic
trees of European temperate forest, such as hazel,
oak and elm, spread quickly and some time
between 7000 and 6500 BC forest on the present
Dartmoor surface reached its fullest extent. It was
then dominated by oak, with smaller amounts of
hazel and elm. Whether it covered all the granite
upland cannot be ascertained from the pollen
record – but even in today's colder and wetter
climate small relict oak woods exist at altitudes of
nearly 1,500 feet, so it is probable that most of the

Moorland Pool, Okement
Valley. There are no
natural lakes on Dartmoor
but small pools do occur
in man-made and natural
hollows.

ground below this altitude was forested, especially where there was shelter Soils formed under this forest which were very similar to the brown earths typically found around Moretonhampstead today – a gritty brown loam with a high content of organic

Valley bog on the Erme Plains, snaking through the peaty gley podsol of the moorland slopes.

matter in its uppermost layers, acid but fertile. This loam is widespread in the drier eastern parts of Dartmoor, and at lower levels throughout the fringes of the national park.

Above the tree line at that time, heath with scattered shrubs would have dominated the plateau surfaces. There is argument about the strict timing and precise causes of the evolution of the pattern we now see from that simple situation. It seems likely that as the rainfall increased and the climate became generally less mild around 6000 BC, blanket bog began to develop where the plateau heath existed. Such peat depends for its formation on lack of both oxygen and the right bases, especially calcium, due to excessive rainfall. Waterlogging of the already leached soils inhibits and eventually precludes the processes which normally break down plant debris and incorporate it with the weathered rock to form soils. So the debris builds up on the mineral surface and carries on its own surface a suite of sphagnum mosses, cotton grasses, rushes and heathers, which become the main constituents of the deepening peat as they die.

As the forest was cleared, early on by natural fires and later by the settlers eager for open space and grazing, so more modification of the soils occurred. Removal of tree cover allowed more rain to strike the surface, and denied the soil its annual quota of potential humus. Leaching increased to the extent of podsol (ashy soil) formation. The leaching out of iron oxides deprives the upper layers of their orange brown colours, leaving them pale grey. The colours deeper down are enriched, and in most places the iron is deposited in a thin crust separating pale grey from orange – the iron pan. If the pan is watertight it causes waterlogging or 'gleying' above it, and thin peat forms above that. This soil – the peaty gley podsol of the soil scientist – surrounds the two great blanket bogs of Dartmoor today in a figure of eight pattern. In detail, it occurs on all the gentle slopes and level spur-tops and benches, and is only missing where valley bogs snake through it on valley bottoms, or where steeper slopes or gravelly clitter sharpen the drainage. It can be seen in many roadside gravel pits such as on Dunnabridge Common, or Merripit Hill between the Warren House Inn and Postbridge.

Thus men began to use the surface resources of Dartmoor and to modify them. Clearing the forest was a shortsighted operation for aspiring farmers who so soon had to learn to conserve their seed corn and their breeding stock. They produced the poorest farming soil we have, but at the same time also produced the moorland we revere for its space, its easy traversal and the remnants of their cultures.

The record preserved in the peat shows that bracken exploded on the Dartmoor scene as the pollen of cultivated crops also increased. Certainly those early farmers cashed in the winnings of the early clearance; excavation of their fields has demonstrated a mole population – and thus earthworm numbers – that cannot survive in the peaty gley podsols now on the same site. Woodland is still where they undoubtedly left it, on the steepest, rockiest valley sides, unusable for other purposes. They used its products, from posts to charcoal, and their successors continued to do that until this century. Deer, foxes and horses also persist, and the salmon and trout of today's Dart are the inheritors of a genetic code that was well established when these early people fished.

In the last 8,000 years or so, man's position in the ecosystem has changed dramatically. Human ingenuity has diminished the environmental constraints enormously. People on Dartmoor, as everywhere else, have become a force for landscape change which is exceptional not so much for its sweeping quality as for the speed with which the changes have been effected.

2 **People before the written record**

Because of the lack of historic record it is easy to lose sight of the individuality and human qualities of prehistoric people and to think that the past was no more than a succession of 'peoples' all doing the same thing day in and day out for so many hundreds of years until their cultures were replaced.

This is a result of the type of material we have available for the study of prehistory, and not of the people themselves.

Even though the edge of Dartmoor sometimes seems to draw a circle of isolation around the granite upland, there are no good cultural historical grounds for regarding Dartmoor as an island. It seems that even the early gathering and hunting people who recolonized Dartmoor after the retreat of the ice sheet, established at the outset a pattern of interdependence between lowland Devon and

Prehistoric peoples exploited the resources of upland areas as well as those of the lowlands. Here at Sharp Tor, 1,254ft (383m) above sea level, the remains of their homes still survive in the landscape.

upland Dartmoor, a situation which persists today. The archaeologist, Roger Jacobi, paints a picture of foragers who made seasonal migrations to exploit resources on both upland and coast. Summer and late summer would probably have been spent hunting red and roe deer, aurochs and wild pigs in the open woodland and clearings around Dartmoor's summits while for the rest of the year the groups moved down to the river estuaries of the south Devon coast to exploit fishing grounds and shellfish beds.

These foragers formed what was arguably a coherent regional population, with its own distinctive culture, judging by the flint and chert tools which it left behind. Finds of these artefacts have been made at a number of coastal and estuary sites, as well as on Dartmoor and other uplands of the South West, but not generally in the lower lands between them; on Dartmoor such sites include East Week near Throwleigh, Ringhill near Postbridge and Moor Hayes on Hayne Down. The distribution of positively identifiable finds is concentrated in the eastern area of the Moor, suggesting perhaps that even at this early stage it was more conducive to human habitation than the exposed western slopes. If modern foraging peoples are relevant examples, we must attribute to the gathering and hunting inhabitants of Dartmoor a detailed knowledge of plants and animals reflecting a closeness of their relationship with the natural world around them. Unlike later farming peoples, the foragers' existence depended on the success of the wild animals and plants which were their food. It seems likely that apart from a little clearance as a result of fire, and the probable domestication of wolves, the foraging people left Dartmoor's natural legacy more or less intact.

Other factors, however, were also at work. Even though the foragers may have been more or less in balance with their setting, that ecosystem itself was vulnerable to a changing climate, as described in the previous chapter. It is clear from pollen analysis that peat formation and resulting souring of the soil was well under way in the higher parts of Dartmoor by 3500 BC when we have the first evidence that agricultural activity was well established. Britain had long since lost its land link with the European continent due to a rise in sea level occurring around 7500 BC when the South West peninsula assumed its present narrower outline. It is assumed (though without much

Spinsters' Rock, Drewsteignton. This Neolithic burial chamber, dating from about 3500–2500BC, probably contained many burials and would originally have been covered by a long earthen mound.

evidence) that knowledge of cultivation and stock husbandry arrived in England via a considerable number of farmer settlers from the continent rather than through being discovered by the aboriginal inhabitants. What became of the latter is not known, but there is no reason to think in terms of annihilation; a fair number, and there were not many to start with, may have adapted to the new way of life, at first co-existing with it, and finally being absorbed in it.

With the coming of agriculture, human beings began to leave traces of themselves which are still visible in the landscape. The period between approximately 4000 BC and the middle of the third millennium BC when the land was first being settled in a permanent way is often called the Neolithic, or New Stone Age. The first evidence of forest clearance in the pollen record comes during this period, and some of the hills may then have assumed their characteristically bare outlines. The barrows at Corringdon Ball and Cuckoo Ball are remains of chambered tombs, and we may assume that these two sites, both well below 1,500 feet, were on ground cleared of forest. There is also a cluster of smaller chambered tombs on Gidleigh Common.

The tombs are, by analogy with other parts of the country, likely to have been communal or family vaults, in which a number of people were successively buried. They originally contained granite chambers, of which Spinsters' Rock near Drewsteignton is the most impressive example, although reconstructed.

It seems odd that in spite of the chambered tombs and flint arrowheads associated with them found at Ringhill and elsewhere, no definite Neolithic settlements have been recognized on the Moor, though they are known in lowland Devon, for instance at Hazard Hill and on Haldon. It may be that with improved dating techniques some of the settlements at present allotted to the second millennium BC will prove to be earlier in origin. On the other hand, the first farmers are likely to have built substantially in timber, which, being so perishable, makes the task of tracing their settlements a difficult one.

On analogy with present-day primitive farming peoples, it is possible that some of these early Dartmoor farmers practised, at least to begin with, wandering cultivation rather than being settled in one spot. This might involve a group clearing a small patch of forest, firing the debris, and using the ash to fertilize cultivation of the cleared area until it became exhausted; it was then time to move on. Soil sections taken from Piles Hill on southern Dartmoor at 1,000 ft (300 m) reveal the presence of charcoal fragments which, together with alder pollen, are good evidence for secondary forest produced by clearing the original oak forest followed by the abandonment of the clearing. There may also have been considerable transhumance or the seasonal movement of livestock between the good upland grazing in summer and the more sheltered environment of valley clearings in winter. But it is probable that permanent settlements were the norm by the time chambered tombs were being built, between 3500 and 2500 BC.

It has been suggested that the Dartmoor chambered tombs, sited as some of them are on the widely visible horizon formed by the edge of higher ground, were built by people who lived in the lowlands, but who carried their dead up to an impressive site for burial. If so it would be another instance of the interdependence of Dartmoor and its surrounding lowlands. It can be argued that whether or not the chambered tombs are linked to the lowlands, some people at this time lived on the

The earliest farmers cleared areas of the original oak woodland and these may have gradually regenerated long after their clearings were abandoned, but by the third millenium BC the rate of disafforestation increased and such regeneration was unlikely.

Moor – after all their forager predecessors and bronze-using successors were happy to do so and the climate underwent no really dramatic fluctuation between times.

As with the foragers, we are more or less ignorant of the culture of the first farmers, though we know from their tools and pottery that they were skilled craftspeople, and excavation of their tombs elsewhere has revealed that their dead were buried with some degree of ritual including libations and animal sacrifice.

From the fourth millenium BC onwards, human beings began to have a radical effect on Dartmoor and became the instrument whereby primeval forest became a managed pastoral landscape.

Some time around the middle of the third millenium BC on Dartmoor, metal-working began to appear, and metal tools gradually superseded the older stone ones. This period is referred to as the Bronze Age, but probably gold was the first metal to be used, followed by copper. Although bronze (a mixture of copper and tin) was undoubtedly important, the use of the conventional term 'Bronze Age' may be misleading.

Ironically it was these first metal-workers who also created Dartmoor's most characteristic prehistoric stone features. The inception of this change used to be attributed to an invasion by the 'Beaker Folk', a 'race' called after a distinctive kind of refined pewter-like pottery associated with the period. In recent years, however, the idea of an invading 'Beaker Folk' bringing metal use with them has fallen into disfavour. It is perhaps better to think in terms of the spread of the idea of a metal-working culture by means of trade contact, which was highly developed throughout Europe by this time.

Much of the pattern of settlement before about 1750 BC remains a mystery. Most of the round burial cairns, as well as the stone circles and probably the stone rows, were already constructed, or were being constructed, at this time; but no contemporary settlements have been confidently identified and we are still more or less ignorant of the function of either the circles or the rows.

Dartmoor's stone rows form a unique collection in terms of density, and the Stall Moor-Greenhill row may be the longest prehistoric stone row in the world. Pollen analysis suggests that some were constructed in what were then forest clearings rather than open moorland.

The purpose of the rows is likely to have been one

of considerable cultural or religious significance, given the labour involved in building the features. Standing in the stone circle of the 'ring cairn' (a type of tomb) on Stall Moor and looking north towards Greenhill along the two miles of stones that comprise Dartmoor's longest stone row, or wandering among the grand complex of rows and cairns at Drizzlecombe, it is impossible to believe otherwise than that the people who built them attached the utmost importance to their function.

This suggests that their purpose was religious and indeed in many cases the rows form approaches to burial cairns. The only common topographical factor about their siting is that they usually lead up to (or down from) a small rise. Most rows are single lines of upright stone, but sometimes the rows are double, as at Hurston Ridge and Assycombe close by, or rarely even triple, as at Yar Tor. The Yar Tor row is in a particularly impressive setting, astride a massive hill overlooking on one side the meeting of the East Dart and Wallabrook Rivers, and on the other that of the East and West Dart Rivers. It is difficult to think of a place more suited to religious observance, centrally situated as it is between the north, south and east upland areas.

Scorhill stone circle in a wild and beautiful setting above the North Teign.

Drizzlecombe menhir. This standing stone terminates a stone row leading from a barrow and stands some fourteen feet above the turf. It is part of a complex prehistoric site with more menhirs, barrows, stone rows and a cist nearby.

This stone row is on the level plain of Long Ash Hill near Merrivale and is part of what may be a prehistoric sanctuary used for burials and ceremonies by several generations.

The stone circles presumably also served a religious purpose. The visual impact of Scorhill stone circle, for example, located near the meeting of the North Teign and its tributary, the Wallabrook, is considerable and it has an individuality that is endowed by its setting in a basin beneath a ring of tors. Indeed, its impressiveness is likely to have been heightened for the ancient visitor with the juxtaposition of oak and alder forest in the lower parts of the basin, and the tors which emerged to contrast the living with the inanimate as starkly as did the presence of people among the stones of the circle. Scorhill is unique among the dozen or so circles on Dartmoor in that it has not been restored; the double circle at Grey Wethers, which is equally impressive, has been considerably reconstructed. Evidence has been found to suggest that ceremonial fires were lit in the centre of the circle, but none of the circles has been found to contain any trace of burial.

Presumably connected with the rows and circles in serving some religious function are the lone menhirs. These solitary standing stones occur less commonly on Dartmoor than might be expected from their frequency in neighbouring Cornwall.

The most striking of them is Beardown Man in a remote setting on the Cowsic River near Devil's Tor. Most commonly they occur in conjunction with the stone rows; as for instance on Shovel Down where the Longstone is associated with a double stone row. At Merrivale, within 494 ft (150 m) of each other, lie a double stone row, a stone circle and a standing stone, although the significance of such configurations is a matter of conjecture. Here too at Merrivale are the remains of cairns and later hut circles.

Many of the cairns dating to the second millennium BC were constructed over cists (rectangular stone chambers), most of them large enough to contain a body interred in a crouched position, but some smaller ones are likely to have contained cremated ashes in pottery vessels. This difference can be seen by comparing (for example) the large cist at Roundy Park near Postbridge with the smaller one on Blackslade Down near Widecombe. The cists were usually sunk into the ground and covered by a large slab. Most have now been opened up and their contents robbed. Some cairns had a retaining stone circle or kerb around the mounds – there is an excellent example at the southern end of the Stall Moor-Green hill stone row mentioned previously; others, known as 'ring cairns', appear never to have had a mound at all, but are defined by a ring of low stones encircling the central burial. Unlike the communal chambered tombs, the cists housed only one burial (though occasionally later burials were inserted within the cairn), and it is assumed that only important people would have been buried there. This suggests the

During the second millenium BC cairns were constructed to cover rectangular stone chambers (cists) in which bodies were buried.

emergence of a social hierarchy with an increase in individual power brought about by a more sophisticated political organization.

The labour involved in the construction of these monuments, particularly the stone rows, must have been considerable, even if aided by some earlier boulder clearance for farming.

It is impossible to consider the start of the metal-using period on the Moor without considering the origins and use of the metal which is characteristic of the age. Dartmoor was rich in its two constituent metals, copper and tin, yet the evidence for their use in prehistoric times is scanty and conflicting. Early metal finds in Devon are thought to have been imported from the Continent, and the current view is that there is little or no evidence of exploitation of Dartmoor's metal resources occurring at this time. Could this really be so? It is often areas which lacked either tin or copper, such as Denmark or Wessex, which are associated with rich metal finds in northern Europe. If the extraordinary concentration of religious monuments on Dartmoor is taken as an indication of wealth of a sort, and wealth did not go with being a producer of the raw materials of bronze, then it seems just possible that the builders of the stone rows on Dartmoor either did not know about, or did not bother to exploit the Moor's metal resources.

In contrast to the enduring ubiquity of their ceremonial monuments, there are few if any positively identified remains of this people's settlements. Very recently, however, a 'platform settlement' similar to those found scooped into hillsides in Northumberland, and possibly dating from as early as 1800 BC, has been discovered at Gold Park near North Bovey by the archaeologist Alex Gibson. This type of dwelling consisted of a circular house set into the hill on one side and supported by an apron of earth – the platform – on the other, to achieve a level living surface. There is evidence that an early timber-framed structure was succeeded by the low wall of stone which is characteristic of later houses.

Speculation about how early metal-using peoples on Dartmoor organized their society, and what effect this organization had on the landscape, is brought into sharp focus by the class of prehistoric remains to have claimed the attention of archaeologists most recently – the reaves. Initially brought to prominence by the pioneering work of Elizabeth Gawne and John Somers Cocks, the

A small cist on Blackslade Down near Widecombe in the Moor.

Dartmoor reaves – low prehistoric stone banks stretching, often in parallel lines, across miles of moor and farmland – have, through the work of the archaeologist, Andrew Fleming, transformed our understanding of Dartmoor during the second millennium BC. No account of the distribution and nature of settlements in this period can be given without first considering the implications of the reave lay-out, whose system, in the cases of Rippon Tor and Dartmeet, extend over several thousand acres.

Reaves are generally unimpressive from the ground. The walker who stumbles across one, say on Yar Tor Down just north of the Dart Gorge, may be aware of a slight rise in the ground stretching in a narrow band to either side, perhaps with gorse or other moorland colonizers of disturbed, raised ground such as heathers.

If the walker were to choose to follow it, he or she might be surprised by its length, often several miles, and its persistence in the face of topographical obstacles such as tors and river valleys. But it is only when viewed from a distance, preferably from the air, in conditions that are just right (sparse snow cover with low sunlight), that the full extent of the reave pattern is apparent. Indeed its recent discovery as a significant and widespread prehistoric feature is more or less the result of aerial photography. In such photographs mile after mile of what seems from the ground open moorland can be seen to have been enclosed in prehistoric times by a well laid-out rectangular system of stone banks.

It is assumed that these reaves were begun a little while after the stone rows and circles were built. Sometimes reaves respect the earlier monuments, as at Scorhill, but at other times they slight them, for instance at Shovel Down. This rather piecemeal approach of the reave builders to the rows and circles has been compared to the development of medieval churches; some of the earlier building commanded respect, but not all. Once again this is evidence for continuity of culture. If the reave builders represented an entirely different race, we might expect either that they would completely disregard the stone rows, or that they would give them all 'fossil' status as sanctuaries of local deities. What has occurred is more indicative of gradual development than sudden change.

Fleming has proposed that the various reave systems represent the potential arable territories of a number of distinct communities around the outer edge of the high plateaux (though there is evidence that reaves on Shaugh Moor may have had a pastoral purpose). The distribution and layout of reaves on Dartmoor suggests careful planning on a large scale. This can be deduced particularly from the phenomenon referred to as 'terminal anticipation', where some of the inner reaves of a system stop short of the terminal reave, suggesting that they were built with a later terminal reave in mind, but their builders slightly misjudged where it would run. It can also be deduced from the way that some systems meet, for instance the Dartmeet and Rippon Tor systems, but also more generally from the fact that the overall pattern suggests a regime of 'inter-commoning' – that is, the use of the upland areas by stock from several different communities together, much as happens today.

Characteristically, a reave system is represented by a number of parallel boundaries, leading towards a long terminal reave at right angles to them, beyond which lies the high ground of the South, North or East Moors, as Fleming refers to them. In the South Moor, as on the River Erme and River Plym, settlements tend to be located in valleys just above the terminal reave, but in the East and North Moors, where the valleys leading into the upland are shallower and shorter, the settlements are often discernible among the reave system. Fleming sees the high degree of organization as best explained by a single political decision taken around 1700 BC, resulting in what he calls a main boundary-making episode.

The reaves of Dartmoor are exceptional among prehistoric field-system remains in their extent and coherence. But does this mean that there was something exceptional about the social organization on Dartmoor of the reave builders? The reaves almost certainly represent the allocation of land to different sectors of a community, possibly families, and the reason why such units went to the trouble of creating so many miles of permanent stone banks that were never perhaps high enough to keep deer out or stock in effectively may be a simple one. We know that some of the earliest reaves were earth banks; these possibly represented initial boundary-marking of areas in which ploughing was to take place. Because of Dartmoor's earlier geological history, with the fragmentation of granite outcrops and the subsequent movement of broad clitter fields downhill towards valley bottoms, ploughing many areas was made difficult by the abundance of stones. In order to plough satisfactorily, even with a shallow implement, the rocks at or near the surface have to be removed. The most natural place to put them would be along the sides of the arable strip (just as the early farmers may have piled stones round the edge of their forest clearings; possible early stone clearance cairns exist at White Hill and Rowter Marsh). Thus they would have achieved clearance and created a permanent boundary in the same operation. It may be that here we see a very direct influence of Dartmoor's geological history on human activity, resulting in a uniquely preserved complex of prehistoric field systems.

Schematic map, simplified of the main Dartmoor reave pattern (after A Fleming).

It used to be thought that second millennium BC settlements on Dartmoor reflected a difference between the south and west and the north and east sides of the Moor. The inhabitants of the south and west sides were supposed to have operated an economy devoted primarily to pastoralism, while those of the north and east sides concentrated on arable farming. This view, put forward by the archaeologist Lady (Aileen) Fox, was supported by the greater frequency of enclosed pounds (settlements with a wall around them) and villages in the south-west quarter of the Moor, by the existence of the field systems around Rippon Tor on its east side, and by the fact that fertile brown-earth soils are more prevalent on this side. More recently, however, the discovery of reave systems in the south-western quarter and the possibility that some pounds there, such as at Trowlesworthy Warren, were in fact cultivated, has called the earlier view into question. It is probably more realistic to think in terms of all the settled areas of Dartmoor containing both pastoral and arable components at this period, and to suppose that stock was pastured in common on the uplands during the summer, and in winter, taken down to fields whose crops had been harvested.

It has even been suggested, by analogy with medieval and later practice, that some people from the lowland South Hams area may have used Dartmoor's uplands for summer grazing, driving their herds and flocks up through narrow droveways like the one still evident at Corringdon Ball near South Brent. Certainly, given the lowland-upland link likely in forager and early farmer times, and recorded from medieval times onward, there is no reason why this should not have been the case in the second millennium BC. The similarity between the map as we have it of the reave-system communities arranged in a ring around the central peat-covered plateaux, and the medieval parish lay-out around the Forest of Dartmoor, often giving parishes access on to the Forest via a narrow tongue, is striking. Just as many of the medieval field boundaries around the high plateaux have followed the course of the prehistoric reaves now fossilized in them (for example just north of Easdon Tor), so the medieval parish layout may represent the Saxon perpetuation of a pattern of settlement and land use that originated in prehistoric times.

The people who built the reaves also left behind them a legacy of their dwellings in the form of circular granite wall bases: the 'hut circles' marked on the Ordnance Survey maps. The Dartmoor expert, Hansford Worth, writing in the first part of this century, knew of at least 1,500 of these ruins, but the actual number is probably near 5,000 and undocumented ones are still being recorded. These round houses had granite walls and a conical thatched roof supported either on a central post or an inner ring of wooden posts. Their doorways faced away from the north west. They were sometimes solitary, sometimes in loose hamlet

Homes have been built on Dartmoor for several thousand years and many traces of them still survive. The earliest structures are the foundations of prehistoric hut circles.

clusters or villages, and sometimes in denser collections encircled by an enclosing wall and referred to as a 'pound'.

Probably the best known collection of prehistoric houses on Dartmoor lies 1,530 ft (470 m) high at Grimspound on the slopes of Hameldown. This now consists of a perimeter wall about nine feet in width, now much restored as regards height but thought to have been six feet high 200 years ago. It encloses the remains of twenty-four small round buildings within an area of nearly four acres, and has an entrance facing south, uphill towards Hameldown Tor. This pound, with its numerous dwellings, was clearly not suitable for cultivation, nor is its position on the slopes of a hill defensible, so presumably it was used as a stock pen. The exposed nature of the site – it faces north west on the north-west slopes of the highest hill in the area – is a reminder to us of three things: first, the sub-Boreal climate was warmer and a little drier than the climate today; second, when Grimspound was built much of the ground below it both to east and west would have been under forest – the brown-earth soils of the two Webburn valleys are a legacy of that; and third that Grimspound is adjacent to one of the most busily

Grimspound, an enclosed prehistoric settlement, lies in a fold in the hills between Hameldown and Hookney Tor and was sited on a small stream, the Grims lake.

Prehistoric house. Evidence for prehistoric settlement abounds on Dartmoor – particularly the foundations of huts. These hut circles consist of a rough circle, from 3–10m in diameter of clearly fifty stones forming a wall with a gap for an entrance which is often flanked by two upright stones, sometimes small or quite large. Originally these walls would have stood a metre or more in height and timbers would probably have been laid from them to a central post – all supporting a roof of wood, turf, heather and bracken. Extra stability was sometimes given by an inner ring of posts.

worked tin-mining areas of historical times on Dartmoor over the Birch Tor emanative centre. Interestingly, a cairn on Hameldown above was the site of Dartmoor's richest archaeological find, a dagger with its pommel pricked out by numerous tiny gold pins. The dagger itself may have been imported, but it had been repaired locally and the repair itself represented a high standard of craftsmanship. Whether there is any link between the settlement at Grimspound and this cairn is uncertain – as we see it today, the pound is probably of a slightly later date than the cairn. But the fact that the dagger should have been found in the area at all could be an indication that the site was an important one, perhaps because of its access to tin, which during the second half of the second millennium BC may have been exploited for local trade.

In spite of the light shed by the discovery of the reave systems, it is still difficult to present a picture of second millennium BC daily life with any confidence. We cannot know exactly what the forces were which led the people to produce the landscape that archaeology and the pollen record suggest they did – an open, partially cultivated upland completely cleared of forest except along some river valleys.

Many of the houses had partially paved floors –
some can be seen at Grimspound. This, together
with the surprising density of dwellings on higher
ground well beyond the reave systems, particularly
on the South Moor, has led Fleming to suggest that
dairying rather than beef was the basis of second
millennium BC farming.

On the cultural side, we know even less about the
religion of the reave builders than we do about that
of the early metal users, who at least erected
religious monuments. Some of the larger burial
cairns probably belong to the reave-building
period, but dating them is difficult. For want of
better evidence we have to assume that the bronze-
using people of the second and first millennium BC
sometimes preserved earlier religious practices
and persisted in using the sanctuaries still standing
from the previous period, much as the post-
medieval people have gone on using medieval
parish churches with some alterations, vandalism
and neglect down to the present.

The landscape on Dartmoor underwent a radical
re-shaping at the hands of people who were
probably eager to produce as much pasture as
possible on the high ground for their dairying. They
had an interest in removing trees both from the high
ground and, for their arable crops, from the more
fertile fringe slopes. The possibilities of trade
probably encouraged them to begin to exploit
alluvial tin, which in turn encouraged settlement
higher up than might otherwise have been the case.
Thus, it is not difficult to understand why these
people would have been keen to remove the forest.

The period from 1000 to 500 BC saw a decline in
the occupation of Dartmoor. There are a number of
possible reasons for this. It may be that the
clearance of forest, which was probably completed
by this time on all the major upland expanses down
to about 1,000 feet, combined with a gradually
deteriorating climate, was having an increasingly
detrimental effect on land productivity. The spread
of blanket peat, which had first made its appearance
on Dartmoor around 4000 BC had reached its fullest
geographical limits by around 700 BC, soils were
becoming poor, and the weather had become
cooler and cloudier. It may be that there was an
increase in sheep at the expense of cattle, as
happened in Wessex, and consequently less labour
was needed on the uplands. Yet there may have
been political reasons too, which we cannot even
guess at.

Holne Chase, high above the River Dart, where a fort built in late prehistoric times may have been occupied by a pastoral people who experienced little threat from 'enemies'.

Later prehistoric settlements include Foales Arrishes near Widecombe, and Metheral and Kestor near Chagford. A prehistoric house ruin at Kestor was excavated by Fox and found to contain evidence of iron-smelting. This has usually been cited as evidence for the continuation of occupation on the Moor into the early iron-using period but more recently it has been suggested that the house could have been re-occupied as a ruin at a later date and used as a shelter for metal-working.

Around 500 BC in other parts of Britain and in the surrounding county of Devon, an iron-working culture became dominant. There was probably some settlement of migrant people bringing this culture into south-eastern England, but the old idea that the Bronze Age was swept away by Celtic invasions now looks less than plausible. Certainly as regards the remote South West peninsula, it is more likely that the culture changed through trade and absorption of new ideas. On Dartmoor, however, the culture did not so much change, as disappear altogether, at any rate as far as discernible remains are concerned. The only identifiable sites from the period between the bronze users and the Saxons of the Dark Ages are the so-called 'forts', usually situated high above the wooded gorges of the perimeter. It is possible that even some of these were begun in the second millennium BC. Their enclosing banks seem to have acted more as stock pounds than as defensible ramparts; though the position of Wooston, Cranbrook and Prestonbury above the Teign Gorge, Hunter's Tor above the Bovey in Lustleigh Cleave, and Holne Chase and Hembury above the Dart Gorge might at first sight tempt speculation about guarding the fastness of Dartmoor from the westward advance of some enemy, which was using the river valleys as a route through the dense oak forest. At present the pattern and function of these settlements is little understood.

Was the upland of Dartmoor completely deserted for nearly a thousand years between the end of the bronze-using period and the end of the Roman period? We know that when the Saxons came they found Celtic people on the Moor – the Dartmoor Saxon river name Wallabrook means 'the stream of the Welsh' (ie foreigners). It seems unlikely that some use was not made of it for most of the period between 500 BC and AD 600 even if only as summer pasture, or as a retreat for people who did not take to the new ways. It may be too that Roman remains on Dartmoor will some day come to light.

But there are two good reasons why occupation as it is known from the second millennium BC should have died out. The first is that the change to an iron-working culture must have undermined the high level of organization which the bronze-using cultures depended on; countrywide, tin and copper are scarce and local resources rely for their dissemination on a complex trade network, which in turn presupposes large-scale political control. Iron on the other hand is widespread and could be manufactured by each group for its own purposes. If some of the settlement on upland Dartmoor in the later second millennium BC was linked to exploitation of tin, and also part of a political system with enough control to plan the reave-system layout, then it may have been affected by the advent of iron-working. The second reason is that around 500 BC a more pronounced worsening of the climate set in with the beginning of the sub-Atlantic period, rendering the high ground of the Moor colder and wetter. It is possible too, that the increasing cold would have killed off the Anopheles mosquitoes along the lower river valleys, and reduced the risk of malaria there, thus depriving Dartmoor of one of its advantages over lowland Devon.

3 The pattern of early settlement

Much of the settlement pattern of present-day Dartmoor has its origins in the Saxon and medieval periods, the basic elements in this pattern being the market and stannary (derived from *stannum*, Latin for tin) towns which fringe the moorland, the small villages sheltering in the river valleys, the scattered hamlets of two or three dwellings and their outbuildings, and isolated farmsteads. Away from the open moorland (once the royal hunting grounds known as the Forest of Dartmoor and later common land) the settlements are surrounded by smallish irregular fields enclosed by hedgebanks and approached by narrow and sometimes sunken lanes. Some settlements, particularly on the higher, marginal areas of the moor have been abandoned, many during the later medieval period, and the ruined buildings and deserted fields form part of Dartmoor's archaeological record – shadowy reflections of a pattern of landscape use which elsewhere has continued unbroken until the present day. On the open moorland, and around and within both abandoned and still-used fields are the visible remains of the tin industry which was so important in Dartmoor's medieval and later periods. Trial pits and gullies are cut into the landscape, and dotted about are the remains of tin mills and other tinners' buildings.

The central area of open moorland is fringed by parishes whose boundaries (those of early estates) it has been suggested were established in the main by at least the seventh century AD. The big, thin parishes of the southern part of the Moor radiate out from the central upland reflecting an economy based upon having equal shares of arable land on the lower slopes and grazing on the higher land. There is some evidence from the pollen record that a certain amount of regeneration of forest had taken place after the retreat of the bronze-using peoples. Indeed it can be argued that the moorland/forest fluctuated until well on into historical times. But any general advance of forest was probably reversed by the time of the Norman Conquest.

There are records of battles fought by the Saxons

against the Celtic 'Dumnonians' of Devon and Cornwall as early as the middle of the seventh century, and by the time Ine and Nunna, the Saxon leaders of Wessex, had defeated Geraint of Dumnonia in 710, colonization must have been well advanced. The degree to which the resettlement of Dartmoor during the years preceding the Conquest was the direct result of the Saxon advance into Devon is unclear, but there is evidence both from a few place-names and a number of Celtic memorial stones found in the vicinity that there was some exploitation of the area in pre-Saxon times. Anglo-Saxon place-names here, as in the rest of Devon, are dominant but this may only reflect a change in administrators and overlordship and the colonization which took place after the eighth century perhaps was merely the continuation on a great scale of a process already begun.

Some religious continuity may certainly have existed. Celtic Christian missionaries from Ireland and Wales had been active in the South West peninsula. On Dartmoor there are two churches dedicated to the Celtic St Petroc, one at Lydford and one at Harford on the River Erme. According to tradition the Saxons of England were converted to

Lydford Castle keep dates to 1195 and was built for the custody of offenders against the Forest and stannary laws. It stands on a mound surrounded by a ditch, which represents part of the site of an eleventh-century castle. But Lydford's history is much longer – it was one of the four burghs of Devon set up by Alfred for defence against the Danes and was one of the four Saxon Mints of Devon.

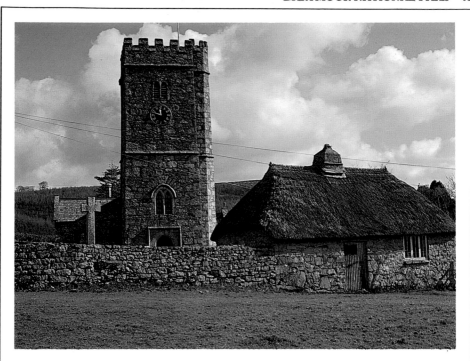

The small church of St Peter, Buckland in the Moor, dates from the fifteenth century, replacing a much older building. Its clock shows letters reading 'My Dear Mother' in place of numerals – a memorial to a local family.

Christianity by missionaries from Rome, but in more remote areas such as the South West they are more likely to have absorbed Christian beliefs from the culture of the indigenous population. A seventh-century Celtic stone memorial has been discovered in Lustleigh church on the east fringe of the Moor; a further eight Celtic stones have been found around the edge of Dartmoor, for example in the parishes of Sourton, Ilsington and Buckland in the Moor, and it is likely that when the Saxons built the churches around which villages grew, they chose sites that already existed as Celtic sacred shrines.

Many of the prehistoric inhabitants of Dartmoor had built their settlements high up on the sides of hills, often in what seem today rather exposed sites; the medieval settlement sites which have survived show a greater liking for valleys, though they are often on small rises within these to avoid the danger of being flooded. Chagford is a good example, set under the surrounding hills but above the River Teign which flows close by. This is indicative of two things: first, that the medieval people were more sensitive to the climate, which had worsened since the days of the reave builders; and second, that the valleys had been cleared of forest during Saxon

times. However, not all early settlements were located in the valleys; many of the hamlets and farmsteads deserted by the thirteenth or fourteenth century are on high ground. The lynchets (terraces produced by ploughing) at Challacombe (around 1,300 feet) are a vivid reminder that early medieval people were also at home on the high moor.

Archaeological investigation of Saxon and medieval activity on Dartmoor has involved the excavation of deserted settlements, for example at Houndtor, Hutholes and Dinna Clerks in the parishes of Manaton and Widecombe in the Moor, and in Okehampton Park, together with the study of field systems such as those on Holne Moor, in Okehampton Park and at Challacombe.

The remains of the medieval hamlet at Houndtor were excavated during the 1960s by Mrs Evonne Minter. This hamlet was set on an east-facing slope overlooking the deep but gentle wooded valley of the Becka Brook. To the north rises the huge, fractured outcrop of Houndtor, while southward lies the less extensive though equally dominating cliff of Greator Rocks. Beyond this barrier, which is partially clothed in woodrush with the occasional rowan and thorn in its crevices, and in May and

Houndtor deserted medieval village. The present surface remains date to AD 1200–1350 but archaeological evidence suggests that a settlement may have been here in the eighth century.

early June lapped by a sea of bluebells, the view extends over one of the rockiest and most imposing of Dartmoor's valley heads with the unique outline of Haytor Rocks on the horizon. The setting, especially if visited on a fine evening in late May or early June when the trees have flushed but before the bracken is up, appears today as a startling mixture of the starkest, strangest and most barren aspects of Dartmoor, combined with other aspects which show it at its gentlest and most fertile.

Assuming this setting was substantially the same in the medieval period, what we know of Houndtor village and its eventual desertion embodies something of the paradox of its surroundings. The substantial remains now visible are those of a cluster of eleven stone buildings – three dwellings and their ancillary structures – that represent the final phase of settlement at Houndtor, from about 1200–1350.

The origins of the site are not entirely clear although the excavator suggested that the stone buildings were superimposed on a long succession of turf-walled dwellings stretching back perhaps as far as the eighth century. Domesday Book records that in 1086 there was a manor of Houndtor belonging to the Abbot of Tavistock, but the identification of this with the deserted site as against, for example, nearby Great Houndtor is unproven.

The open ground surrounding the site of Houndtor and the smaller settlement (known as Houndtor II) to the north is still moderately fertile; just below, oak is vigorously colonizing open moorland, and bracken, always a good indicator of well drained and productive ground on Dartmoor, was ubiquitous before it was killed by recent spraying. An east-facing slope, protected by a ridge from the north west and west, well drained and yet relatively gentle, already cleared of forest and rocks by prehistoric settlement in the area, must have presented a good site for occupation. Though it gives an impression of height, the site of Houndtor village is not far above the 1,000 ft (304 m) contour, not especially high by medieval or even present-day standards on East Dartmoor; for example nearby Natsworthy, a settlement mentioned in Domesday Book, is sited at 1,250 ft (385 m).

The inhabitants of Houndtor would have practised a mixed agricultural economy. Recent analysis of pollen from the sites indicates that in the thirteenth century cereal crops, including oats and rye, were being grown in the area, and over the down, south and west of the sites, can be seen the remains of the small sub-rectangular fields belonging to the settlement, and (in suitable light) the 'ridge and furrow' left by medieval ploughing. Further evidence of cereal growing comes from the presence of kilns built into three of the outbuildings on the main site, which were used to dry corn.

At the settlement site itself, the visible remains are of three principal dwellings, known as 'longhouses' (home to both humans and animals), one subsidiary dwelling and seven outbuildings. (See also Chapter 5.)

The outbuildings probably served a variety of purposes – further housing of cows or draught animals, dairies or storage of produce and equipment. Three of the buildings at Houndtor have inserted kilns and areas used to dry corn. Small enclosures surrounding the settlement were probably used as kitchen gardens or animal pens.

Why was this hamlet deserted in the mid-fourteenth century, along with Houndtor farmstead a little way to the north, and never re-occupied? The documentary record is silent on this. Guy Beresford, who wrote up Mrs Minter's excavations, suggests it was because of the climatic deterioration known to have set in by this time and the need to dry corn artificially at Houndtor is certainly evidence of a wetter climate. At other now-deserted sites on the Moor, for example Hutholes near Dockwell in

Theoretical reconstruction of an early medieval longhouse based on archaeological excavation. The early type of longhouse was of single-room depth crossed by a central passage on the upper side of which was the living area and on the lower a shippon for cattle. Animals and people would share the same entrance. The roof was of thatch. These buildings were single-storey and open to the roof and had a drain with an outlet in the gable wall. Most standing, occupied longhouses surviving today are of slightly later origin.

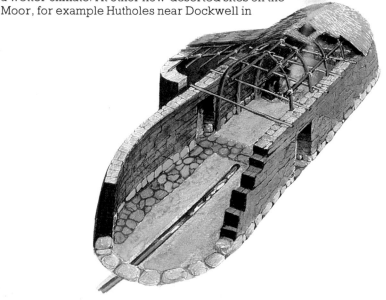

Houndtor, steeped in
history, lore and legend.

Widecombe, it appears that the population of the
settlement was decreasing prior to final desertion,
for buildings that had once been houses were
turned into barns. A similar shrinkage seems to
have occurred at the hamlet of Challacombe two
miles to the north, although here the process of
desertion was arrested and the site which once had
at least seven dwellings is now occupied by a
farmhouse and a couple of cottages. From what
evidence we have the picture seems to be one of
gradual desertion and abandonment of those areas
which had become marginal.

It may possibly be that the Black Death, which
arrived in England in 1348, contributed towards the
desertion of some sites. Plague would have spread
through the tightly clustered dwellings very quickly
once it had entered them, and perhaps some upland
settlements were not thought worth the trouble of
re-occupation because of developments of farming
practice, which came with the change from an open-
field communal farming system to the more
individual system of private management that has
persisted since later medieval times.

There are many deserted sites scattered
throughout the Moor, ranging in size from the
hamlets like Houndtor, Blackaton (thirteen
buildings) or Hutholes (nine buildings) down to
single farmsteads such as Dinna Clerks on the
eastern slopes of Corndon Down. The shape and
size of the buildings on these sites is similar to those
found at Houndtor and the longhouse especially
should be comparatively easy to recognize.

Within Okehampton Park, lying to the south of the
town, are scattered the remains of a number of small

medieval settlements of a type already described –
single longhouses with or without barns – or groups
of dwellings linked to each other and their enclosed
fields by hollowed trackways. Excavation here has
suggested that the land was first taken into
cultivation and settled in the late twelfth or early
thirteenth century; at one site timber buildings
were first constructed but these were translated into
stone and more added during the thirteenth
century. Desertion of all the settlements was
however brought about suddenly when the area
was cleared of its inhabitants at the end of the
thirteenth century and turned into a deer park for
the use of the Courtenays when resident at
Okehampton Castle.

Today's farmed
landscape in the Bovey
Valley.

All but one of the settlement sites belonging to the
community which farmed Holne Moor from about
the ninth to fifteenth century are unlocated and may
be beneath the Venford Reservoir. The one
remaining longhouse site lies just south west of the
reservoir itself, just inside the Water Authority
paling. The Holne Moor fields, like Houndtor, are
set on an east-facing hillside at between 1,000 and
1,100 ft (304–334 m) overlooking the Dart Gorge. As
at Houndtor, they are on ground previously
enclosed in prehistoric times. In contrast to the well-
planned cohesive system of the prehistoric reaves,
the first pre-Conquest enclosures at Holne were laid
out in lobes – rounded enclosures projecting from a
central focus.

These lobes (the most complete surviving one is
some thirty acres in size) date to the tenth century or
earlier and were subdivided into a number of fields
used mostly for arable cultivation, although there
are small areas of pasture within them. The fields
themselves are further subdivided by banks or
lynchets into cultivation strips each on average just
over an acre in extent, and it may be here that we
have evidence for the 'open-field system' on
Dartmoor. In such a system land was held
communally by a number of tenant farmers who
each, in order to ensure fair distribution of good
and bad land, cultivated a number of small strips (of
about an acre) scattered throughout the field. After
cropping, the fields could be used for communal
grazing, and the strips could be reallocated at the
beginning of each growing season. The
inconvenience of such a system eventually
outweighed its advantages and tenants or landlords
would arrange to swap and amalgamate a number
of strips and enclose them permanently; on

Holne Moor: Medieval
Field System (after A
Fleming and N Ralph).

occasion they even enclosed ordinary strips. The period at which this enclosure happened varies throughout Devon from (where datable) the thirteenth to fifteenth century, although one open field is still being cultivated today in strips at Braunton in North Devon. Not all land was cultivated by the open-field method and some fields have probably always been enclosed and held individually, although open fields were more common in Devon than was once thought. The long thin curving fields to the north of Lydford (whose pattern is clear on the Ordnance Survey $2\frac{1}{2}$ in map) are probably enclosed strips, as are those at Dunstone in Widecombe in the Moor, or around Michelcombe and Scorriton in Holne. At Challacombe, north of Widecombe, where the strip lynchets along the valley sides are clearly visible from the road, the land appears to have been worked in parcels well into the seventeenth century.

The establishment of the Royal Forest, possibly in the eleventh century, as a royal hunting ground prevented expansion by the Holne Moor farmers on to the open ground west of the lobes. At this time the field walls defining the lobes were converted to corn ditches – ditches of asymmetrical section which allowed deer to pass from field to Forest with ease, but (on the whole) prevented them from escaping from Forest to field.

In 1239 Dartmoor was removed from Forest Law almost certainly as a result of pressure to bring more land under cultivation. Central Dartmoor was granted by the Crown to the Earl of Cornwall and became technically a chase (the hunting domain of the nobility), though it continued to be known as the Forest of Dartmoor. At Holne Moor the disafforestation was followed by a period of expansion in which moorland to the west was enclosed, at first on a small scale, but finally taking in a larger area than the original lobes. These areas are known as 'outfields' being used only for casual and intermittent cultivation as opposed to the 'infield' which was cultivated on a more regular basis. The open moor was at this time being increasingly used for sheep grazing in response to the burgeoning wool trade. This expansion had a brief lease of life and in the fourteenth and fifteenth centuries it was allowed to revert to open moorland. At the same time the original lobes were gradually being turned over to pasture, arable cultivation ceasing altogether around the end of the fifteenth century.

The use of Dartmoor for grazing stock had its origins far back in prehistoric times.

By the sixteenth and seventeenth centuries, farming at Holne Moor had been discontinued and tinners had invaded the ground with their workings, breaking down boundaries where these were in the way and robbing them to make artificial rabbit burrows, known as pillow mounds. While tin-working and rabbit warrening went together on Dartmoor, these two activities on a large scale are clearly incompatible with arable farming, and the presence of pillow mounds in conjunction with the disruption of wall banks must indicate the end of cultivation.

The general picture of settlement so far outlined is one of colonization during the centuries preceding the Conquest, followed by expansion, particularly in the twelfth to early fourteenth centuries and contraction and desertion during the later fourteenth and fifteenth centuries. It is however a tendency for archaeological study to concentrate on those sites and areas which have 'failed' and it must be said that many medieval settlements on Dartmoor have continued in use until the present day. The majority of the sixty or so Domesday place-names in the area of the national park are attached to sites or settlements still in occupation. Other sites, such as perhaps Colwichtown in Cornwood parish which belong to the post-Conquest expansion are also working farms today.

In early medieval times, the division of the Dartmoor area into an inner zone comprising the two high plateaux known as the Forest of Dartmoor, and an outer fringing zone known as the Commons of Devon, was well established. As we have seen in the previous chapter, the use of parts of Dartmoor by lowlanders with stock probably had its origins far back in prehistoric times. All of Devon (excluding, for reasons unknown, the boroughs of Totnes and Barnstaple) enjoyed rights of common on any of Dartmoor's unenclosed land that was not in the Forest, emphasizing the strong link between upland and lowland, and the important part played by the Moor in Devon's economy. In turn the fringing parishes in which the Commons of Devon lay had farms in them with rights of common in the Forest itself, known as 'venville rights' – originally *'fines villarum'* – denoting the fact that an annual charge was levied for the privilege. This is likely to have been a Norman tax on an ancient custom, since the early charters relating to the Forest make a point of preserving rights of common as already practised. Such a custom has been inscribed on the

Swallerton Gate, Houndtor. Dwelling sites in this area have been occupied and then deserted and re-occupied in later centuries. Some dwellings have had a long, relatively unbroken and varied occupancy, such as this house which has been a farm and in the last 150 years a cider-house, a farm again, an afternoon tea-house and private dwelling.

Dartmoor landscape in the form of the boundary stones of the fringing parish layout, where the parishes are shaped to give them access to the Forest parish of Lydford. Extreme examples of this shaping have led to the long corridors of Ugborough, Harford, Throwleigh and Manaton.

The emphasis on commoning that all this implies reflects the importance attached to being able to remove stock, principally cattle, from potential arable ground during the summer months. As it had been with the reave builders, arable farming was a dominating force behind the pattern of early medieval settlement which laid down the outline of today's picture on the Moor.

Within the Forest itself, along the valleys of the two Dart Rivers, lie the thirty-five Ancient Tenements, completing the pattern of early settlement. These valleys provide relatively sheltered micro-climates, for the most part at altitudes not greatly above the 1,000 ft (304 m) contour which is often quoted as a height above which habitation on Dartmoor becomes marginal. Evidence for their antiquity lies in the fact that they were held as copyhold, a form of tenure which could only exist if it had been custom time out of mind when first entered in the roll of the Manor court. They were largely on land which had been enclosed by the reave builders as part of the Dartmeet and Stannon reave systems, thus presumably already partially cleared of rocks and without trees – an attractive prospect to settlers. The fields surrounding these tenements have a regularity reminiscent of Celtic field patterns and in these remote areas, the possibility of continuity with some sort of Celtic occupancy is not improbable. The tenants of the Ancient Tenements – whose population almost doubled in the first half of the fourteenth century – were privileged under a forest custom to enclose another eight acres from the Moor whenever a new tenant took over. It seems that a local interpretation was eight acres of good new land, and those acres might be scattered among a larger acreage of poor stuff. This came to be regarded as an abuse of the system by the Duchy during the seventeenth century, but despite its concern customary 'newtaking' of this kind continued into the eighteenth century.

The first record of the Ancient Tenements occurs in 1260 when the occupants of two of them, Babeny and Pizwell, petitioned Bishop Bronescombe to be allowed to use Widecombe rather than Lydford church for burial and the sacraments since the route to Lydford was eight, or in bad weather, fifteen miles longer than that to Widecombe and involved crossing the central part of the Moor. Their request, which may have had something to do with the rising prominence of Widecombe, was granted. But the funeral trek across the Moor to Lydford, along a track called (after a word for corpses) the 'Lich Way', still easily traceable in the vicinity of the Cowsic River, passed into Dartmoor's cultural consciousness as a symbol of the importance of the ancient borough of Lydford.

Domesday Book recorded Lydford as one of only five towns or boroughs in Devon. Built by the Saxons as a defensive centre against Danish raids, its streets were laid out on a regular system – an example of early town planning. The Saxon defensive bank can still be seen across the neck of the promontory and the existing street pattern is that of the original borough. Excavations carried out within the town over the past two decades have identified the property boundaries (fences and ditches) of the Saxon settlement, and traces of timber buildings. The town, which was Crown property, became the centre of administration of the

Lustleigh, a small compact village which developed around the church. The attractive and individual architecture of its domestic buildings ranges from fifteenth- to sixteenth-century granite and thatch to present-day styles.

Sheepstor church and village cross. This granite church, dedication unknown, was mostly rebuilt in the early sixteenth century, and has a fine tower with crocketed polygonal pinnacles. The origin of the Sheepstor cross is uncertain.

law of the Forest of Dartmoor, and also the seat of the stannary (tinners') court and prison in Lydford Castle.

However, Lydford's origins and history are not typical of Dartmoor's towns and villages. Most of the nucleated settlements on and around the Moor probably had humble beginnings, as farms or small hamlets which expanded to become centres of administration, trade, industry and religion. Some centres, for example Sampford Spiney or Sheepstor, never grew much beyond hamlet size although each had a church and was the religious focus for its area. Other settlements grew into villages, like Widecombe, Christow or Peter Tavy, providing various services for the surrounding countryside: churches, inns, smithing for instance. The reasons why one location should be favoured for expansion over another are various; some are strategically placed on important routeways on, to, and around the Moor – Widecombe again, or Mary Tavy adjacent to the way between Tavistock and Okehampton, others are sited in sheltered valley situations or near rivers and streams or perhaps even near sites of mineral (tin) wealth. Today many of the Dartmoor villages still have good examples of domestic peasant buildings from the sixteenth to eighteenth centuries – in granite at Lustleigh, Shaugh Prior and Throwleigh, or in white-washed cob at Dunsford.

The change from village to town was normally

associated with an official change in status to market town or borough. The Lord of the Manor would apply for a licence or charter from the Crown to hold a market at a specific site, which would give that settlement a particular status and function in relation to its surrounding area. Along with the granting of charters and holding of markets came trading links with other centres, economic wealth and commercial success. Merchants would settle in the newly created towns and build houses for themselves, and their presence would encourage others, shopkeepers and artisans, to settle in their wake. Market towns on and around Dartmoor were Tavistock, Okehampton, Bovey Tracey, Chagford, Moretonhampstead, Ashburton, Buckfastleigh, South Brent and Lydford. Okehampton was virtually created by Baldwin, Sheriff of Devon, as part of William the Conqueror's strategy for keeping the rebellious people of Devon under control. It was the building of the castle which led to the development of the settlement which itself soon acquired borough status.

Another small town which differed from the norm was South Zeal on the northern side of Dartmoor. This was a borough created (with market and fair) in about 1264 by the Lord of the Manor of South Tawton, with the intention, it is thought, of capturing trade from travellers on the then Moretonhampstead to Okehampton road. South Zeal is a planned town, planned in one phase on a virgin site to the south of South Tawton. With houses fronting on to the main street and long narrow ribbons of land, known as 'burgage plots' extending behind them, at right angles to that main street, the whole town is contained within an area of 84 acres. The foundations of South Zeal have been described as 'optimistic speculation' – speculation which was never realized, for South Zeal never caught-on as an urban centre. What we can see there today are, for the loss of a few boundaries, the fossilized remains of a fourteenth-century town uncluttered by the later expansion and additions which characterize the other moorland centres.

For several of the new Dartmoor towns, growth was assured by the emergence of a booming tin industry in the latter half of the twelfth century. Chagford, Ashburton and Tavistock, all previously market towns, were designated as 'stannary towns' for the collection and coinage of tin in 1305, and in 1328 Plympton also acquired that status. The decline in the tin industry around the sixteenth century did

Nun's or Siward's Cross, a medieval bound cross and, standing at over seven feet in height, an important waymark.

Former stannary town, a long-established market town and in the last 120 years a moorland 'resort', Chagford is still an important centre for the farming communities around.

not bring about a decay in the towns, for by then they were also sharing in the general prosperity of the woollen industry. This first rose to significance in the thirteenth and fourteenth centuries and continued intermittently down to the nineteenth century. The wool was generally spun in farmhouses and cottages on the moors and brought down to the market towns for 'fulling' or 'tucking', cleaning and milling. The mills which carried out these processes used the water provided by the rivers running off the moors. Clearly towns with a good river or stream (Ashburton and Buckfastleigh for example) were in the best position to take advantage of water power for mills to process the wool.

The medieval pattern of towns, villages, hamlets and farms lay within the administrative and religious framework of estates, manors and parishes. Little is known of the estates of the pre-Conquest period, although a couple of charters survive describing the bounds of two late Saxon estates, one at Meavy and another in the Ashburton-Widecombe area, and others are being recognized, together with even older land units, in the course of archaeological research. The manorial system described in Domesday Book, divided the land into units (manors), often smaller than parishes, but sharing parts of their boundaries, at the centre of which would have been the manor house and/or home (or 'barton') farm. In North Bovey parish for example, manors were centred at North Bovey itself, Beetor and Shapley; land that was not being worked directly from the home farm would have been let (for money or service rent) to tenant

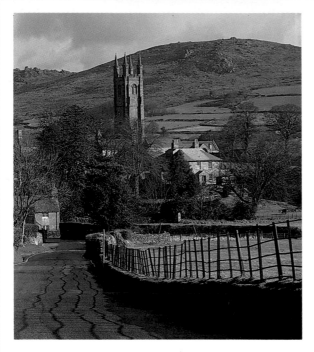

Widecombe in the Moor lies within the sweeping vale of the East Webburn River and here the dramatic rock forms of Chinkwell and Honeybag Tors dominate the skyline. The farms in the area have probably existed in one form or another on their present sites since Saxon times.

farmers (known as 'villeins' in Domesday Book) and many farms and hamlets on Dartmoor today must be standing on the sites of the homes of these tenants.

The boundaries of some parishes may have been established as early as the seventh century, having their origins as early estate bounds. By the thirteenth century (at the latest), each parish had its own church although there is evidence for earlier Christian sites at a number of places, including Buckland Monachorum and Lustleigh. Many of the medieval churches to be seen today are associated with the focal settlement, village or town, of a parish; Chagford, Ashburton, Widecombe and Lustleigh are good examples. In other parishes where there was no large settlement, such as Sampford Spiney or Harford, the church often stands next to the manor house or barton farm.

In a few cases (Walkhampton, Brentor, Buckfastleigh) the church was built a little way from the communities it served and it may be that such churches, when not associated with adjacent deserted settlements, are rooted to ancient holy places. Brentor, a small, mostly thirteenth-century church has a particularly interesting position standing alone on a cone of volcanic rock within the

St Pancras church, Widecombe in the Moor. The so-called 'cathedral of the moor' dominates the village. It was built in the fourteenth century on the site of an earlier church and then was enlarged and the 120ft tower added in the fifteenth or early sixteenth century. The magnificence of the tower is attributed to the financial support of tin miners who exploited all the surrounding valley for the rich ore.

ramparts of a prehistoric defensive enclosure. In so many parishes the basic pattern of settlement and church established in the medieval period has endured without fundamental change until today.

The Dartmoor churches, as in the rest of the country, were reflections of the wealth or poverty of their parishioners; most on Dartmoor were rebuilt or enlarged during the fifteenth and sixteenth centuries when the tin and wool industries were at their height and the dominant architecture is of the Perpendicular period. Some traces of earlier building periods do survive, for example, parts of what were once cruciform churches (possibly fourteenth-century) at Ilsington, Holne and Widecombe, and Norman work at Meavy and South Brent, but generally it is the Perpendicular form of low nave with one or two aisles and a sturdy western tower that is most often seen. The church builders were somewhat hampered by the available stone, for granite is not easily carved into decorative motifs, and the impression of the Dartmoor style is often one of austerity, relieved to some extent by the addition of external stair turrets to the towers and crocketed pinnacles, especially in the north and north west of the Moor. Widecombe church probably most fully represents what the fifteenth-century builders on Dartmoor were trying to achieve, and indeed it has been called the 'cathedral of the moor'. Inside the churches, again because of the use of granite, arcades tend to be fairly plain with simple capitals, but, where it survives, for example at Buckland in the Moor, Christow, Throwleigh or Chagford, the detailed and skilful carving of the woodwork in the screens and bench ends is compensation.

Churches, of course, were not the only physical expression of religious faith in the medieval period. On the edge of the Moor three of the great abbeys of Devon – Tavistock, Buckland and Buckfast – flourished. Both Tavistock and Buckfast were founded before the Norman Conquest, the former, a Benedictine house, received its charter as early as 981. In 1137 Buckfast was taken over by the Cistercians, the great sheep farming order, who also founded a new abbey at Buckland in 1278. All three sites were dissolved by Henry VIII in the late 1530s and passed into private hands. Buckfast was again refounded and largely rebuilt by a community of Benedictine monks at the beginning of this century and is still a living, working, praying monastery.

Lying so close to the Moor, the abbeys naturally looked to it as a source of income and owned considerable tracts of land there. Buckfast and Tavistock in particular sent sheep on to the moors and took part in the rise of the local cloth industry during the thirteenth and fourteenth centuries. The excavations carried out by Lady (Aileen) Fox at Dean Moor – a site now submerged by the Avon Dam Reservoir – suggested that here was a small medieval homestead (house, yard and byre) used by the lay brothers of Buckfast Abbey during the thirteenth and fourteenth centuries while depasturing animals on the open moor. The settlement was deserted around the time of the Black Death.

The monks are reputed to have been responsible for the defining and marking of tracks across the Moor. But it seems likely that many of the routes linking major settlements or providing access to and across the Moor were in existence in early medieval times. Indeed, for all we know, some may have followed prehistoric trackways. Clapper bridges on these routes, such as are to be seen at Postbridge, Dartmeet and less obvious locations, were probably first constructed in the thirteenth century, with large single slabs of granite spanning the gap between short piers. This form of bridge continued to be constructed down to the nineteenth

Buckfast Abbey. The present abbey church was consecrated in 1932, some 900 years after its original foundation. The new church and monastery was built by monks of a community of French Benedictines.

Below Statue of the Madonna and Child, Buckfast Abbey.

Teignbridge clapper bridge. Clapper bridges on Dartmoor were probably first constructed in the thirteenth century and continued to be built in this form until the nineteenth century. The original bridge here was swept away in a flood in 1826 and was immediately reconstructed resulting in the structure we see today.

century. Also belonging to the thirteenth and later (ie fourteenth and fifteenth centuries) are wayside crosses which provided landmarks to guide travellers across the Moor. Among the earliest recorded crosses is Siward's or Nun's Cross just west of Foxtor Mires, and examples from later periods can be seen at Hele Cross in North Bovey and West Week in South Tawton. Some of the early routes are still major routeways like the road from Moretonhampstead to Two Bridges; others have escaped transition into tarmac. The so-called Abbots Way crosses the Moor in a rather tortuous way from Buckfast to Tavistock (the monastic connection giving it the name), but just to the north of it is another and easier route marked by a line of crosses, which may have been called the Maltern Way. Other well known tracks include the Lich Way, mentioned earlier, between the Ancient Tenements and Lydford; Sandy Way, leading out on to the Moor from Michelcombe near Holne; and an ancient track from Ashburton to Tavistock. This latter route was marked (probably at the end of the seventeenth century) by a series of guide stones, inscribed with the letters 'A' on one side and 'T' on the other. Some of these can still be seen at Merrivale between the prehistoric stone rows and Yellowmeade, and occasionally re-used in nearby gateposts.

4 **The tin industry**

Down the centuries the Dartmoor resource has influenced ways of making a living outside the ordinary run of rural life. It seems probable that the tin industry on Dartmoor was already old by the time of the Norman Conquest. But tin-working had a broader influence on the moorland, altering the physical and cultural environment in other ways.

The early tinners extracted the tin ore, called cassiterite, from alluvial beds by means of a process known as 'streaming'. This involved turning over the gravels along valley bottoms and using water to wash and sort the heavy tin ore from other lighter minerals. Retaining walls and parallel ridges were constructed to channel the flow of water, traces of which can be seen at sites such as Skit Bottom on the East Okement and Brimbrook near Cranmere Pool. A good supply of water was essential and streams

In most Dartmoor valleys are remains of tin streaming, the process by which early tinners extracted tin ore from alluvial beds.

were diverted for the purpose, or even on occasion straightened to increase the rate of flow. The East Dart at Sandy Hole Pass has undergone this treatment, likewise the Wallabrook near Scorhill. The humpy terrain now evident along so many Dartmoor valleys bears testimony to the ubiquity of the early tinners' search, as do the common Dartmoor field-names 'Pitts' and 'Stannets' (from the same root as 'stannary').

To begin with, the ore was crushed by pestle and mortar and melted twice, first of all on the spot in a crude furnace consisting of little more than a hole in the ground to produce a coarse ingot, and then again at the place of assay to refine it for taxation and sale. By the end of the thirteenth century the introduction of water-powered tin mills, which both crushed the ore and worked bellows directed into well built furnaces, meant that only one smelting was necessary due to the consequent improvement in the process.

The tin mills have left some of the most fascinating medieval remains to be seen on Dartmoor today. They embody the height of medieval industry and, now in ruins, seem in complete harmony with their present distinctly rural surroundings, because they were built with and used materials from the ground around them. They were rectangular structures of granite, then known as moorstone, and roofed with thatch. A leat (a man-made water course) brought the water to an overshot wheel housed in a wheel pit beside the mill building, where it turned a shaft which passed through the wall of the mill to power bellows and crushing equipment inside. Birch Tor and Vitifer mine leats and those associated with workings at Eylesbarrow are well worth tracing to their source. A leat operates exclusively by gravity flow and a keen sense of the lie of the land was needed by the leat surveyor. Leat cutting can be regarded as a vernacular craft as the work was usually entrusted to local tinners who were the experts. Mine-leating systems are inevitably more complex than those of drinking-water leats due to the fluctuations of closure and re-opening of mines. Mortar stones, with single, double and triple hollows where they have been pounded by stamps, can be seen *in situ* in some of the ruins, such as at Nosworthy Bridge on the left bank of the River Meavy near Burrator. Mould stones, in which the liquid tin from the furnace was cooled and set into ingots, are also in evidence at a number of sites.

It is reckoned that for a period in the twelfth

century Dartmoor was probably the leading tin-producing area in Europe, though Cornwall was soon to overtake it. Such intensity of mining and smelting activity could not avoid influencing other aspects of life on and around Dartmoor. Many of the ruined stone huts that can still be found on the high ground of the central part of the Moor are likely to have served as dwellings for people engaged in tin streaming.

Tin extraction from Dartmoor must have encouraged a higher density of settlement on its fringes than would otherwise have been the case. The four stannary towns on the edge at the Moor, where tin was taken to be assayed, weighed and taxed, owed their growth to the tin industry, which also probably helped to pay for the enlargement and rebuilding of many moorland churches,

Medieval tin mill. A small waterwheel-powered stamping machine for crushing tin ore to a fine sand and also bellows for providing a forced draught for a smelting furnace. Water for the wheel was brought in an artificial leat taken from the river further upstream. The stamps were raised and dropped by the rotating action of the extended axles of the waterwheel. A stream of water then passed the crushed material through a grate and into a settling pit where the first concentration of the tin took place. After more settling processes the fine 'black' tin was ready for smelting in the blast furnace. The smelting operation continued for about 12 hours after which the molten white tin was tapped off into a trough from which it was ladled into a granite ingot mould.

Medieval tin streaming gave way to lode-working, a technique involving digging gullies into hillsides to extract the tin. Such remains are particularly extensive in the Headland Warren and Birch Tor area.

particularly in the fifteenth and early sixteenth centuries. The tinner's emblem of rabbits in a circle can be seen in carved roof bosses in Widecombe and North Bovey churches.

On the high moorland tin extraction perhaps acted as a considerable brake on agricultural expansion. The charters of King John in 1201 and Edward I in 1305 expressly confirm the ancient rights of the tinners to search for tin and otherwise to go about their business (eg divert streams, take wood for faggots, and dig peat) anywhere without penalty. The tinners were to be considered part of the Royal demesne or farm, and therefore exempt from the normal processes of justice, being answerable only to the courts of the stannary organization. This would have proved a powerful disincentive to any kind of agricultural enclosure in areas where tin-working was prevalent, generally on the high moorland – the excavation on Holne Moor suggests the damage that tin-working could do to farming land. The jurisdiction of Lydford, with its royal connection and its feared stannary prison, over the central plateaux must have also played a part in keeping these expanses more or less free of enclosures until the eighteenth century.

During the thirteenth and fourteenth centuries tin production on Dartmoor subsided somewhat from its heyday in the twelfth century. As alluvial tin became harder to find, streaming gradually gave way to lode-working, a technique which involved following lodes of tin still *in situ* in the parent rock by digging gullies, some of them up to 100 feet in depth. Such gullies can usefully be visualized as linear quarries. Lode-workings have also left their mark in the form of place-names ending in Beam, such as Cater's Beam or Scudley Beam – the word 'Beam' very often indicates a past lode-working.

Along with this change in technique (perhaps partly caused by it) came a second boom in Dartmoor's production, though it never again matched the Cornish output. Between 1450 and 1495, production doubled, and doubled again between 1495 and 1515 to reach a peak in the 1520s. In 1521 Dartmoor's mines produced 280 tons of tin. The gullies and gerts (the local name for a large gully) which went with lode-working, and the reservoirs which were often built to provide water for it, for example on the west side of the River Taw near Steeperton Tor, have had a considerable effect on the detailed topography of parts of Dartmoor. Tin streaming and lode-working together have probably done more to alter the relief of Dartmoor's unenclosed ground than anything else since the Ice Age, but just as the industrial tin mills seem as if they had grown out of the landscape, so the alteration effected by open-cast tin mining was of the same order as the natural processes of weathering and erosion. That Dartmoor could have been so heavily industrialized by medieval standards, and yet today be referred to as 'the last wilderness in southern England', regarded as a semi-natural island in a sea of human domination, is a striking indicator of the difference in scale between medieval and modern industry.

The tinners themselves were a mixed bunch. It was never clear exactly who were entitled to call themselves by the term; some did so only when it suited them. Broadly speaking, from the later medieval period onward there were three levels of tinner: the dealer who was often based in London, the local merchant who organized the distribution of the refined metal and the man who worked the mine. It is the last that usually springs to mind in considering the tin industry on Dartmoor, but it should not be forgotten that, especially in later times, the miner was working under direction from the merchant, who himself depended ultimately on the dealer.

Evidence about the conditions of a tin miner's life is conflicting. On the one hand they have been depicted by writers such as Hooker in the sixteenth century and Westcote in the seventeenth century as desperate men, working for a pittance under the most appalling conditions. On the other hand in early times, unlike the serfs on the manors around them, they were technically free men, and were notorious at that period for the number of holidays they took. They also enjoyed the protection of the Crown in their mining enterprises, and exemption from prosecution under ordinary law may have provided a considerable incentive. Being a tinner not only qualified a man for exemption from the normal course of law, but that he was able to bring anyone who stood in his way to the stannary courts.

The statutory independence of the tinners is well symbolized by the fact that, over and above the ordinary stannary courts held in the stannary towns, twenty-four representatives from the four stannary districts occasionally convened a stannary parliament. There is a reference to such a parliament as early as 1474, and there were probably others earlier still. Between 1474 and 1786 there were thirteen known meetings of the parliament, most of them assembling at Crockern Tor in the centre of Dartmoor, where seats, since removed or destroyed, were reputed to have been carved out of the granite for the purpose. The tinners' intimate association with central Dartmoor is reflected in the popular term for them, 'The Old Men of the Moor'.

Methodist Chapel, Poundsgate. John and Charles Wesley began their Devon missionary endeavours in 1743 and met with little success. It was only in the middle decades of the nineteenth century that Methodism took a hold.

The stannary organization included the more extensive Cornish mining operations, which linked Dartmoor with Cornwall. This link has continued, the chapel worship prevalent in Cornwall taking a strong hold on the Moor in the nineteenth century, fostered by the influx of miners from Cornwall who were summoned to contribute their expertise to Dartmoor's third mining boom. Though the mining there was not for tin, the arrival of Cornish miners in Bridford parish during the first half of the nineteenth century is documented in James O'Hea's study of the Upper Teign Valley at this period.

This third mining boom was, like the second, the result of developments in mining technique which rendered previously untapped sources of tin ore accessible to profitable exploitation. Although a few shaft mines were operating on the Moor as early as the sixteenth century – Furze Hill near Horrabridge being one such – it required the development of explosives and pumping equipment to bring shaft mines into their own. Most of the nineteenth-century mines were shaft mines, following lodes underground. They were almost always sunk on the sites of former beam works (Bachelor's Hall mine being a notable exception). Connected with the vertical shafts and the adits which tunnelled horizontally into the hillside to give easier access, were a number of surface buildings whose ruins exist in various states of decay. Large wheels known as engine wheels, powered by water from leats, were sited at some distance from the shafts and used a flat-rod system to operate machinery for pumping and raising ore. The remains of such a system are still discernible at Eylesbarrow. Dressing floors with square and circular buddles for separating out the ore are visible at several sites. A building above West Coombe connected with the East Vitifer shaft mine in North Bovey parish was a house for storing gunpowder. Other ruined buildings which are too small to have been mills probably housed miners.

For the nineteenth-century mining episode, we have records of where some of the tinners lived and details of their families. For instance, the census of 1841 records that at Hatchwell in Widecombe parish and not far from the Birch Tor-Vitifer and Golden Dagger mining complex, three of the four households contained men engaged in tin mining.

Tin mining continued at certain sites, notably Hexworthy, Golden Dagger, and Birch Tor-Vitifer, well into the present century. There are people still alive at the time of writing who can remember going

Blowing house,
Nosworthy Bridge.

underground to work these mines. Despite the advent of steam and combustion engines, they generally continued to use Dartmoor's age-old form of natural energy, water power; the Birch Tor-Vitifer leat drove around twenty wheels for pumping and crushing. At Hexworthy, water was used to generate electricity, which then powered the machinery.

Though the shaft mines of the last mining boom did succeed in extracting a significant amount of tin – the Birch Tor area alone produced some 187 tons of refined tin in 1864 – many of them were ventures which obtained their funds and spent their proceeds elsewhere. They tended, like much Victorian enterprise on Dartmoor, to be highly speculative and relatively short-lived. As such, though they provided a good deal of local employment, their effect on the community was far less than that of the earlier mining booms. Whereas even the churchwardens of Chagford, as recorded in their accounts, had invested in the medieval tin industry, there is little evidence of community involvement in the nineteenth and twentieth centuries.

5 Farming

Dartmoor shares with the other upland areas of Britain a distinctive farmhouse type, the longhouse, which provided accommodation for humans and animals under one roof. This is different from the standard Devon farmhouse or 'hall house', which was also divided by a cross-passage, but where the lower end was given over to domestic purposes (service rooms), never to house animals. These two types of building are probably coeval but represent distinct traditions, although many of the later modifications and alterations were common to both. The distribution of the longhouse in Devon, is, with a few exceptions, confined to the area of the national park; the Devon farmhouse appears throughout the county and sometimes, particularly in the north-eastern parishes of Dartmoor, as neighbour to the longhouse.

The tradition of building houses of the longhouse type persisted into the late medieval period on Dartmoor and many of those which are still standing (and often inhabited) appear to date from the fourteenth to seventeenth centuries. Within these longhouses, as with the earlier excavated examples, the upper (human) end, open to its thatched roof, was often subdivided into two rooms, the main room or 'hall' being heated by a central hearth. Smoke from this hearth hung about in the roof space, and smoke-blackened roof timbers and thatch still survive in a number of longhouses, as at Higher Tor and Uppacott near Poundsgate. The shippons (cow houses) are characterized by a central drain, slit windows, a dung hole and holes marking the position of tethering posts; they would have been partially floored, with large beams carrying a hayloft.

The sixteenth and seventeenth centuries saw much alteration and some rebuilding. In almost all longhouses the hearth in the hall was replaced by a chimney stack, usually sited with its back against the cross-passage, and additional space was created by the insertion of a first floor in the upper end; sometimes this development was staggered so that the end or inner room might be floored whilst the

Shilstone, Throwleigh, a Dartmoor longhouse. The present building dates to 1656. In this building the house part lies to the left. Animals have entrance to the shippon by a door alongside the house door; an entrance from the lobby to the shippon gave access to cattle without the necessity of leaving the building.

hall was still open to the roof. Granite porches were sometimes added, also outshots (which are single storey additions along the side of the house, sharing the same roof pitch) and occasionally entire wings. The longhouse varied in the degree of sophistication from site to site; towards the lower end of the scale are places like Higher Uppacott, a relatively simple building with origins and development as outlined above. Sanders in Lettaford represents a more elaborate house with large granite ashlar work and a single-storey porch, but is still a plain and undecorated structure. At the other end are buildings which have separate doors to the shippon end (whilst retaining the cross-passage access), two-storey porches, granite door frames carved in low relief, mullioned windows or fine ashlar masonry. Internally too, there is some degree of decoration, with chamfered and stopped wooden screens, beams or lintels in most of the houses, but with more elaborate ornamental features in the greater ones, such as arch bracing in the roof trusses or moulded and carved granite fireplace surrounds.

Some effort, skill and money must have gone into creating the more prestigious buildings such as Shilstone in Throwleigh, Chittleford in Widecombe, or Hole Farm, Chagford. The affluence represented by these buildings must have resulted from the booms in the wool and perhaps also the tin industries. The wealth which inspired and funded the rebuilding and enlarging of parish churches may also have found expression in some of the domestic buildings of the Moor.

Although it might be assumed that the longhouse

An old granite slotted gatepost, now redundant as a modern gate replaces the former timber rails.

arrangement contained all the elements of the farmyard within four walls, it is rarely, if ever, that longhouses are found in isolation. Most of the early excavated sites were found to have separate ancillary buildings, and this is also true of the later standing examples. Sanders has a small barn behind, thought to be contemporary with the building, and at Shilstone there is a seventeenth-century barn and linhay, with later pigsty, stable and dungpit. Many of the specialist farm buildings and features seen today (where not obviously modern) belong to the eighteenth or nineteenth centuries. These might include, together with those already mentioned, shippons, pound houses (where the cider was made), ashhouses, walled gardens, cobbled yards, pot-water leats and stone troughs. A number of other useful additions to the farm, such as slotted gate posts for timber rails, were built and carved with extraordinary skill from the difficult challenge of obdurate moorstone. Thus the natural desire for improvement, combined with the means to achieve it, was channelled by a buoyant Elizabethan culture into Dartmoor's greatest period, and the one from which its finest and most typical extant buildings date.

Towards the end of the eighteenth century however, improvement on farms began to mean something different. The Forest of Dartmoor, which for so long had remained the domain of tinners and commoners, suddenly became the theatre of intense agricultural activity. Improved communications provided by the development of the turnpike roads, combined with a nascent appreciation of some of the more spectacular parts of Dartmoor as scenery, had begun to attract members of the emerging gentry class. An optimistic belief in the application of scientific ideas to the challenge of agriculture led several to buy land on the high Moor and to obtain grants from the Duchy of Cornwall to enclose large areas of what had previously been common land. The modern village of Postbridge was more or less founded as a result of one such enclosure. But this was a small event by comparison with what was to follow.

Towards the end of the eighteenth century a few people saw the opportunity for agricultural improvement on Dartmoor with consequential effects on the landscape; some changes however, were subtle, hardly noticeable.

The career of one man expresses the change in mentality among people with power over Dartmoor. That man was Thomas Tyrwhitt, who originated from Essex. While at Oxford University he had befriended the Prince of Wales, the Duke of Cornwall. He made use of his subsequent position as

the Prince's private secretary to set himself up on Dartmoor in 1785 at a place he built just south of Two Bridges and called Tor Royal. His ambition was to transform the high plateaux of Dartmoor, which in his eyes appeared useless waste, into a great prairie growing cereals and grass. This was to be done by dint of hard work and the application of the latest scientific methods, in the process providing

employment for the community he had founded on a strangely exposed site at 1,300 ft (395 m) between North and South Hessary Tors called Prince's Town in honour of his patron.

In the event, though he was later made Lord Warden of the Stannaries, and had every available power at his disposal to do with the Forest of Dartmoor as he wished, his grand design to convert it into farmland largely failed. He had to sell his estate at Tor Royal, and died a broken man. But in casting about for some way of turning his desolate Princetown (as it was afterwards called) into a thriving centre for enterprise, he had hit on the idea of promoting a prison there to house prisoners from the Napoleonic wars. The prison was duly built, using granite from nearby quarries created for the purpose, and though it closed down after the cessation of hostilities, the buildings remained. Later in the nineteenth century, after Tyrwhitt's death, the need for civil prisons occasioned the reopening of the prison at Princetown, ensuring the survival of the settlement there. Likewise a railway to Princetown which he had initiated was constructed, albeit uneconomically, and remained in operation until the 1950s – its course can still be

Dartmoor Prison, Princetown. Lying in the middle of Dartmoor this little town lies some 1,400ft (319m) above sea level with a harsh climate of mist, wind, snow and rain. The town and prison owe their existence to one man, Sir Thomas Tyrwhitt, who, towards the end of the eighteenth century, set about exploiting the 'wastes' of high Dartmoor.

traced. Single-handed, Thomas Tyrwhitt had originated the most unlikely, yet the largest settlement served by the best communications on upland Dartmoor.

Tyrwhitt's kind of estate management on a large scale was and is foreign to Dartmoor and Devon in general, where the tradition of the small farmer has been particularly strong. Tyrwhitt himself came from an area of the country where the large feudal estate with its own village is a characteristic feature, and this is what he tried to recreate on Dartmoor. But he underestimated the difficulties presented by the climate and the soil, which combine to make large areas of central Dartmoor a poor growing environment without drainage on a massive scale, the application of huge quantities of fertilizer, and improved crop varieties. He also cut across the ancient common rights of the Forest tenants and the venville farms (farms with common rights on the Moor) of the surrounding parishes by enclosing land within the Forest, which cannot have made him popular. Altogether, he failed to understand and respect the land he colonized, and was only able to go as far as he did because he had the Prince of Wales's ear.

The surrounding commons and their parishes remained more or less untouched either by the enclosures that were taking place in so many other parts of the country, or by the spirit of scientific optimism and capitalist enterprise which drove Tyrwhitt and his kind. The slowly evolved and well-tried system of village, small farm, and common was resistant to outside 'improvement' of the sort described above. Not for the first or last time, established human settlement of an area provided the best safeguard against violent change.

This is not to say that Dartmoor farming away from the Forest remained static. Farming and its associated industries, in particular the wool industry, had grown more dependent on markets as self-sufficiency decreased and money became more important. The rise of sheep farming in the fifteenth and sixteenth centuries occasioned the conversion of smaller field boundaries into the massive wall-banks which guard most of Dartmoor's valley fields today, planted with trees like hawthorn, blackthorn, ash or holly to make a sheep-proof barrier. But the rise of sheep farming was itself determined by the expansion of Devon's wool trade, the prominence of which the ardent traveller Celia Fiennes witnessed and vividly described on her visit to Exeter in the

The main gateway, Dartmoor Prison, carries the words '*parcere subjectis*' – to spare the vanquished.

1690s. The cottages of Dartmoor's villages which give the impression of having grown up around their parish church probably grew up just as much around their local water mill which processed the wool that people in the cottages had spun and woven. There were tucking (fulling) mills in Chagford and Moretonhampstead as early as the thirteenth century.

This all changed, however, during the nineteenth century with the coming of the Industrial Revolution and the collapse of the market for wool. The clothing industry was snatched out of cottages all over the land, including those on Dartmoor, and gathered into the industrial centres of the North. Different localities of Dartmoor were hit at different times. Records for the parish of Bridford show a peak for poor relief claimed in the year 1820 almost certainly connected with the collapse of its cottage wool industry. But new machinery in the Ashburton mills enabled clothiers there to compete well into the middle of the nineteenth century.

Farming generally went through a depression in the wake of the Napoleonic wars, which had kept market prices artificially high. In response to this, farming on Dartmoor, as documented by the diaries of the Reverend Robert Palk Carrington, vicar of Bridford, underwent a revolution comparable with that which has occurred since the Second World War. Farming methods that today we regard as traditional, such as the use of draft horses, and the growing of root crops in place of fallow, were the products of this revolution, just as are the large high corn barns with round houses attached where draft animals revolved to power threshing machinery – a good example of a Victorian corn barn of this type exists at Oldbrook near Buckfastleigh. Wheeled vehicles too were virtually unknown on Dartmoor before the middle of the nineteenth century – Carrington remarks on the first wheeled carts in Bridford in 1842. Up till then, owing to the poor state of the roads, carrying was done by pack animals, often donkeys, and sledges were used on farms. A double packhorse stile can be seen across a lane west of Rowbrook Farm above the Dart Gorge.

With the aid of technological innovations of this radical but unalarming sort, farming recovered to become relatively prosperous again by the middle of the nineteenth century. Perhaps partly as a consequence, the population of many moorland parishes reached a zenith at this time, and the last large-scale building phase commenced. A

The North Bovey Valley
with its scattered farms,
hamlets and village from
Hunter's Tor.

considerable number of Dartmoor's cottages date
from this period, and new farmhouses, though
usually on old sites, were also erected. Widecombe
parish, Grendon, Blackaton Manor, Bag Park,
Wooder and Natsworthy all have Victorian farm or
manor houses on or near the site of earlier
settlements, in most cases with attached cottages.
They were put up by a second generation of well-to-
do improvers, generally less ambitious than the
first. A glance at the modern map of Grendon and
Blackaton Manor, however, is enough to show that
the urge to impose a scientific regularity on the
landscape had not passed with the eighteenth
century. The extreme linearity of the field layout,
which even extends to the straightening of the West
Webburn River, was the work of Frederick West,
who removed all the previous boundaries in order
to achieve it. Like Tyrwhitt before him, he went
bankrupt, but like Tyrwhitt too, his imprint still
remains in the landscape.

 During the eighteenth century a number of the
Ancient Tenements fell into the hands of one or two
new, wealthy and powerful occupiers, as the Duchy
appeared to lose interest in the Forest. By 1780 the
'newtaking' custom was being adapted by these

new improvers, and the Duchy aided and abetted the new enclosing process, by making grants to enclose very large areas of the Forest. By this means new farm holdings, even small 'estates', extended the original enclosed landscape right across the basin of the East and West Dart Rivers, and physically divided the open Forest land into two, with the small islands of Dunnabridge Common and Riddon Ridge lying inside this great swathe of 'newtakes' and farmsteads. The improvers were also responsible for the construction of the two turnpikes, which join at Two Bridges, and whose prime practical purpose was the servicing of the new farms.

Within the same period, various landowners whose property bordered Dartmoor proper, were granted enclosure powers either by the Duchy, or by specific Acts of Parliament. So 'newtakes' also appeared – so suddenly on occasion as to surprise the parish worthies – in places like Ilsington and North Bovey in the east, and Peter Tavy and Walkhampton in the west.

Nevertheless, by this time a number of constraints on such arrogant treatment of the land had begun to appear. One was the farming depression of the 1870s and 1880s, from which arable farming on Dartmoor has never really recovered. Another was a growing awareness that Dartmoor's value went beyond its agricultural and mineral potential, and that its archaeological heritage in particular needed to be safeguarded. This resulted in the formation of the Dartmoor Preservation Association (DPA) in 1883. The original stated aims of the Association had been enlarged to include not only the protection of rights of way and common rights but also the preservation of antiquities. These original aims are still in the forefront of the DPA's work though land-use conflicts in the twentieth century have necessitated other stances. The DPA is still a very effective voice for the retention of Dartmoor so that future generations may enjoy it.

In the present century Dartmoor has remained sheltered from the most dramatic visual effects of changes in farming practice, which have largely come about since the area was designated a national park in 1951. This, combined with the fact that many of the developments have a limited application in the uplands, has afforded a degree of protection and helped to continue the brake on the pace of change which the granite environment had previously applied. Nevertheless, the consequences of mechanization even on a small scale have been to reduce the agricultural labour force and to cause holdings to be amalgamated, sometimes leading to the desertion and ruin of farmhouses and other dwellings. Cripdon Farm near Manaton is a typical example – now in an advanced state of decay, it was occupied within living memory.

Whatever changes there have been in agricultural practice, subtle or otherwise, some traditions have been maintained, the most apparent of these being the keeping of herds of ponies on the open common. For centuries, and probably from prehistoric times, the indigenous ponies of Dartmoor have provided a strong and reliable workforce for farmers and miners and for those hauling granite or carrying peat, wool, timber, lime and other commodities.

At the beginning of this century there was a demand for ponies small and strong enough to work down the coal mines of Wales, the Midlands and the North. Shetlands were introduced on to Dartmoor and the resulting smaller cross breeds were sent away in thousands to the pits. This was the first time the Dartmoor ponies had been exported in any

Ponies have been kept on the moor for centuries. Today only a few thousand remain, the need for them having declined in this mechanized age, and their hardiness having been bred out has made out-wintering on the Moor more difficult and costly.

numbers. Nowadays, the farmers who rear ponies do not have a use for them on the land, except perhaps riding out over the moors to check their stock. And so most of the ponies, other than breeding mares, are sold at the five or so pony markets around the Moor – a few are sold to horse-riders, but most are bought by the meat trade.

Because of the introduction of different breeds, only a few of the original extremely hardy Dartmoors are left (mainly on stud farms), and the present ponies on Dartmoor, not being as hardy, do not always come through the tough Dartmoor winter in good fettle. Moreover, there are no subsidies on ponies as there are for hill farmers on cattle and sheep, so the profit per head of pony is minimal. Fifty years ago there were 25,000 ponies on Dartmoor but in recent years there have been less than 5,000. While a decline in numbers was inevitable in this mechanized age, it is to be hoped that it is worth the Dartmoor farmers' while to continue to keep these animals which seem to depict the essence of Dartmoor.

6 **The influence of other industries**

Industries of many other sorts have played a part in the life of Dartmoor since the Saxon colonization. Some of these were centred on the villages, and often, like cloth making, depended on the products of farming for which they provided a considerable market. For example, in the year 1800 one-third of people living in Moretonhampstead were engaged in manufacturing activities such as curing and tanning leather, tallow making, rope and paper production, as well as the more important clothing industry. James O'Hea has shown that the proportion of people occupied in trades, manufacturing and handicrafts in the Upper Teign Valley increased at the expense of agriculture between 1811 and 1851, even though the bottom had fallen out of the wool market.

Such industry helped to preserve and even

Most of the major Dartmoor rivers run off the Moor through steep-sided, densely wooded valleys. The woods are typically broad-leaved and mostly coppice oak – a reminder of Dartmoor's industrial past where the produce was used for tanning and charcoal.

enhance the structure of the Dartmoor villages and towns; these same villages and towns suffered badly from rural depopulation in the first half of the twentieth century, when the coming of good roads accompanied by the motor vehicle made it more economic to centralize and concentrate production regardless of the location of the consumers.

Peat, oakwoods and water have all played their part in the many industries which have been associated with Dartmoor historically. Peat, burnt directly or converted to charcoal, was used in smelting systems; it has always been a domestic fuel, and at various times in the last 150 years has been used to distil naphtha and petrol, and for horticultural and paper-making purposes. Coppiced oakwoods produced charcoal and tanning bark in large quantities for tanyards at Okehampton, Moretonhampstead, Horrabridge, Tavistock and Sticklepath. Water, as a source of power, was crucial to all industry here and another factor in the removal of small-scale village industry from Dartmoor was the abandonment, towards the end of the nineteenth century, of water as a source of power. Leats are numerous on Dartmoor and were constructed to 'lead' water for all its many purposes historically. As well as providing water for industrial activities many were built for domestic purposes – whether for solitary farms and fields or for much larger domestic water schemes. The earliest scheme was completed in 1597 – Drake's Leat which starts from a weir on the Meavy near Sheepstor and across Roborough Down, and runs for seventeen miles to Plymouth. When this project was first proposed in 1560 it was inevitable that expert advice was sought from a tinner. With some improvements, Drake's Leat was to remain Plymouth's water supply for another three centuries.

Water is now in demand for all the needs of a growing population well away from the hills where it falls in great abundance. The building of reservoirs on Dartmoor was inevitable and the first moorland reservoir to be constructed was Burrator in 1898, subsequently enlarged in 1928. There are now eight reservoirs supplying the Torbay towns, Newton Abbot and Teignmouth, as well as the South Hams and large areas of north-west Devon.

One unusual industry using water power and set right in the middle of the Moor was the gunpowder factory at Powder Mills, established in 1844 by George Frean. Its isolation was due to the need to

Powder Mills, near Postbridge, where during the latter half of the nineteenth century gunpowder was manufactured. Water power and building stone were easily available and unlimited space enabled the various processing buildings to be dispersed – reducing the potential danger of spreading fires and explosions.

test the powder without endangering or deafening neighbouring inhabitants. The present hamlet at Powder Mills owes its origins to the now defunct factory, whose remains are very well preserved and make a fascinating testimonial to the way Dartmoor scaled down even Victorian industry to blend in with its surroundings.

Water power was also used for the copper and other mineral mines not concerned with tin which sprang up around the periphery of Dartmoor largely in the nineteenth century. They were mostly on the metamorphic aureole, where the lower crystallization temperature of their minerals had led to them being deposited further from the hot granite than tin. Copper for instance was mined at Mary Tavy and in the Dart Gorge near Holne Bridge; lead and silver at Wheal Betsy near Peter Tavy; arsenic at Stormsdown and Owlacombe; iron at Haytor and barytes near Bridford. Micaceous haematite, a form of iron ore used unsmelted in anti-corrosive paints, was mined quite extensively on the granite around Hennock and the Wray valley. The Great Rock mine was working until 1969 and had employed as many as twenty-seven people in its workforce just before the Second World War. Many of these ventures, however, like their Victorian tin counterparts, were short-lived, and it is doubtful whether, apart from the immigration of Cornish miners they brought with them, they had any significant effect on settlement.

The two nineteenth-century ventures with a more lasting influence were the quarrying of Dartmoor granite on a commercial scale, and the extraction of china clay. Undressed surface granite had been used by people from at least as far back as the building of the chambered tombs; from medieval times the same surface granite was split by wedges and dressed with axes. Clearly, with so much so readily to hand, there can have been little incentive to quarry the stone. Nevertheless many churches and medieval longhouses are testimony to the fact that the moorstone was well worked by masons and outside decoration achieved in this difficult medium. By the nineteenth century, however, more sophisticated demands in volume were made. Quarrying, in the form that we now recognize it, was probably begun at Haytor by George Templer sometime between 1800 and 1820. The remarkable granite-railed tramway which carried the blocks down to the Stover canal can still be seen in place over a considerable distance beneath the tor. Granite from the quarries there was used in the rebuilding of London Bridge and for the British Museum. Granite from the five quarries around Foggin and King Tors established by Thomas Tyrwhitt built Dartmoor Prison and continued to be extracted up until 1937. The quarry at Merrivale, however, established in 1876, is still operating, and the settlement there, though not as large as it was, owes something of its present existence to quarrying. This quarry dealt with the cleaning and repairing of Old London Bridge before it was shipped to Arizona for re-assembly in 1970.

China clay, the product of 'kaolinization' of the granite, was first mined on Dartmoor in earnest by William Phillips, who acquired the tenancy of the Lee Moor pit in 1833. As with so many eighteenth- and nineteenth-century adventurers on Dartmoor, Phillips died a ruined man; but the Lee Moor pit has survived to become one of the largest clay pits in the world. Outposts of the nineteenth-century working in the Avon and Erme Valleys are long abandoned

Today china clay constitutes Dartmoor's only industrial product which can be called of national importance, and the village of Lee Moor was literally created out of empty moorland to house its workforce, once again largely of Cornish origin. The scale of the present china-clay working in Dartmoor's south-west corner strikingly points up the relative smallness of all Dartmoor's historical industries and demonstrates how different modern industrial practice has become. Clay is won by high-pressure hoses and thus the handling of water controls the depths of pits and ensures their horizontal extension. Not only is the depth of the kaolin unknown, but methods of extraction at depth still elude the industry.

Warrening and peat-cutting were two ways of making a living which were responsible for some of the most isolated dwellings on Dartmoor from medieval times to the present century, and for some distinctive markings of its terrain. Warrening was for a long time closely associated with the tinners, who kept rabbits to feed themselves and for fur. But it was also an activity in its own right, and there were large warrens at Trowlesworthy Warren, Ditsworthy Warren, Huntingdon Warren and Headland Warren among others, which though they were established in tin-mining areas, continued independently of the tinners in later years. The ruined warren house at Ditsworthy, which was occupied in the present century, gives a good idea of the isolation of the warrener's existence, set in the valleys of the upland Plym with no other sign of human habitation in sight. This was necessitated by the potential damage rabbits might cause to farmland. On the hillside behind it lie some of the man-made cigar-shaped pillow mounds in which the rabbits had their burrows. Warrens had rabbit-proof walls and usually were delineated by boundary stones.

Many of the ruined huts on the high Moor were occupied at one time or another by peat-cutters – for example Mute's Inn at over 1,900 ft (577 m) near the top of Whitehorse Hill. Peat was much in demand by the tinners to make peat charcoal for smelting, but it has always been a source of domestic fuel as well. The peat 'ties', the scars of peat-cutting, are widespread in the blanket-bog area and in the larger valley bogs. Peat, too, has occasionally been the subject of larger-scale commercial enterprise; in 1846 land was leased near Holming Beam with the intention of extracting peat there to be converted into naphtha in part of the Princetown prison buildings. The project did not last longer than a year.

In 1586 William Camden had written of *'squalida montana*, Dartmoor', which more or less means what it sounds as though it means. Obviously, as long as Dartmoor conjured up reactions of this sort it was unlikely to become a tourist attraction. In those days, if we are to believe the Elizabethan and Jacobean poets, the Thames Valley around London provided the landscape ideal for the English sensibility. The poet Robert Herrick, who was rector of Dean Prior during the seventeenth century, wrote nothing about Dartmoor, and only mentioned Devon to complain of its dullness.

But as industrialization destroyed the attractions of areas around the cities, people began to look further afield to places whose landscape, though in fact far more ecologically degraded than the Thames Valley type had been, still provided the sense of contact with nature prized by the Romantic movement developing around the turn of the eighteenth century. Dartmoor was such a place, and from this time onwards tourism began to play a part in its cultural consciousness and its economy. The hotels at Postbridge and Two Bridges are essentially products of nineteenth-century tourism pioneered on the upland by men such as William

Higher Stiniel – a typical Dartmoor hamlet surrounded by farmland. Such scenes reflect a long historical continuity and are valued today for their beauty and serenity.

Crossing, author of the famous *Guide*, published by *The Western Morning News* in 1909. Born in Plymouth in 1847, William Crossing was the leading Dartmoor authority during his lifetime. He kept careful records of his Dartmoor excursions and studies, and wrote prodigiously for local papers, mostly about Dartmoor. A series of articles in *The Western Morning News* was eventually published by David and Charles in 1966 under the title

Dartmoor's landscape provides enjoyment to some eight million visitors a year.

Crossing's Dartmoor Worker. This depicts the ethos of Edwardian Dartmoor through those whose livelihoods depended on the Moor including the peat-cutter, the warrener, miner, clay labourer, quarryman and wall builder and Crossing also wrote about the visitor, the artist and the guide.

From the outset of the Romantic movement, art and literature had been instrumental in creating the change in sensibility which, combined with improving communications, led to Britain's uplands becoming tourist attractions. But owing to the powerful influence of the French and German Romantics, Alpine scenery became the early model for the sublime in nature. The Lake District, as most clearly resembling this kind of landscape in Britain, was already popular when William Wordsworth began to write. The influence of Wordsworth and other Romantics on English artistic consciousness of the nineteenth century effectively meant that artists who painted Dartmoor, including J M W Turner, chose the gorges and cleaves of the periphery where, from certain angles, the prospect could be made to look mountainous, or at least spectacular. Meanwhile the poet Nicholas Carrington wrote of

'Devonia's Alps'. This description could hardly be more inappropriate in geological, ecological, topographical or human terms, but such an attitude contributed to the early preferences for places such as Lustleigh Cleave as tourist spots, served as they were by the railways opening up around the periphery. Some of those who visited were charmed enough to want to settle or at least build holiday houses, and Victorian villas sprang up in Lustleigh, Belstone, Okehampton and Ashburton, all on railway lines. Yelverton too was virtually created as a holiday resort town through the railway.

But another town on the fringes never had the benefit of either a railway line or even a good road, and yet still managed to become a tourist attraction. It is in the history of Chagford, as documented by Jane Hayter Hames, that the effect of nineteenth-century tourism on a settlement can be seen to best effect. Chagford's wool mill closed in 1848, and the agricultural depression of the 1870s and 1880s did nothing to improve the employment situation. Nevertheless, the then rector of the parish, Hayter George Hames, had a sewage system laid, gas lighting was introduced at his instigation, and finally Chagford became the first town west of London to be lit by electricity, which was generated from the wheel of the old wool mill. Meanwhile Hayter George Hames was busy publicizing Chagford as a pleasant place to visit, with the result that artists and the gentry began to flock there and hotels sprang up. Without any longer possessing any significant industry, Chagford was able to keep and even improve its former stature.

In the twentieth century, the close proximity of the large conurbations of Plymouth, Torbay and Exeter, combined with improved roads and faster cars, has made commuting to work from Dartmoor ever more feasible. The increase in commuting has led to housing development in desirable areas such as the towns and villages on the fringes of the Moor, development which is unconnected to local employment. This is perhaps one reason why, whereas the population of most upland areas in Britain declined between the censuses of 1951 and 1971, that within Dartmoor National Park increased by ten per cent.

The same factors that led to housing development also helped to increase the use of Dartmoor for recreational purposes in the late twentieth century. Southern Devonians had long regarded 'the Moors' as a regular visit – whether it was the bus trip from

Lustleigh Cleave has been a popular beauty spot for over a century. It is part of a fault system which extends along the edge of north-eastern Dartmoor. The lines of weakness in this area allowed weathering processes to dissect the land deeply and so expose the underlying granite.

The National Parks and Access to the Countryside Act 1949, recognized that 'those extensive tracts of country which by virtue of their natural beauty, the opportunities which they afford for open-air recreation, their character and their position in relation to centres of population should be designated as National Parks'; Dartmoor was designated as such in 1951.

Newton Abbot to Widecombe, the weekend ride to Burrator or Roborough Down from Plymouth or the early morning trek into the high plateaux from the railway station at Lydford, now long closed. In the 1980s, sixty-six per cent of the eight million visits a year are made to the national park by Devonian residents. They have their popular and regular target sites and there are a number of heavily used popular sites in the park – more in the east than the west – most associated with water, though there are exceptions including Haytor, Roborough Down and Widecombe-in-the-Moor. The National Park Authority tries to make sure that these popular places can cope with numbers, do not deteriorate, and remain satisfying to their regular visitors.

7 **Plants and animals**

As an environment for plants and animals, Dartmoor is surprisingly singular. It is the largest and highest area of upland in southern Britain, and this combined with the relatively low intensity of agricultural practice in recent years, has led to a surprisingly wide range of species surviving. Many upland species thrive in the cold, wet climate and southern and south-western species survive rigorous conditions because this upland is so far south. Environmental influences are overlain by human activity, reflected in the presence on Dartmoor of many species which are scarce in much of lowland England but can still be found here in abundance where farming is basically pastoral.

These influences on the flora and fauna can be traced in the distribution patterns of many species – northern plants such as crowberry can be found on the high plateaux of Dartmoor whilst bastard balm, a species of central and southern Europe, grows on the fringes of the moor. Pale butterwort, found in many local valley bogs, has a 'Lusitanian' distribution, typically along the coasts of France, Spain and Portugal, and in the extreme west and south west of the British Isles. Sub-arctic lichens such as *Umbilicaria torrefacta* may be found on higher moorland boulders a few hundred feet above woodland trees draped with 'old man's beard' whose European distribution is now virtually restricted to Brittany and south-west England' (largely because of air pollution in the north and east).

Rare upland birds such as golden plover and dunlin breed on Dartmoor's blanket bog and are the most southerly in the world, whereas Continental species at the northern edge of their range such as woodlark can be found breeding around the moorland fringes.

All these species contribute to the ecological richness and variety of the Dartmoor ecosystem which has been recognized by the designation of a number of Sites of Special Scientific Interest (SSSIs), national nature reserves and other local reserves. The habitats which make up this ecosystem are

In the absence of proper human control the instability of heather and grass moorland is manifested in the ease with which it is invaded by bracken, one of the world's most successful invasive plants.

broadly divisible into open moorland, broad-leaved woodland, conifer plantations, enclosed farmland and rivers and riverbanks. None of these habitats is strictly 'natural' and all have been affected by human activity – the first two have been modified by man whilst plantations and farmland have been entirely created by man.

Open moorland encompasses a complex of vegetation types which reflect, as everywhere, underlying environmental factors overlain by past and present human management. Today, grazing and burning maintain that treeless character so beloved by those seeking wilderness and solitude.

Blanket bog which covers the highest slopes (generally anywhere above the 1,500 ft (457 m) contour) is composed of a thick layer of peat, often several yards thick and laid down over thousands of years. It is this peat 'sponge' with its immense water-retaining capacity that feeds Devon rivers.

Pools and hags, hummocks and hollows now criss-cross its surface, making walking difficult but providing a micro-climate for the few species that can survive in this wild, high place. Bog-cotton, with its distinctive fluffy white tassels in early summer and long narrow winter-red leaves, dominates much of the vegetation together with deer-grass, rushes, sedges and bog mosses (principally sphagnum species).

Drier slopes and hummocks support heathers (ling and cross-leaved heath) with whortleberry, tormentil and milkwort. Particularly on the southern Moor, vast tracts of blanket bog are dominated by purple moor grass with its raffia-like golden leaves. Few other species are found – perhaps the result of too-frequent burning. It is on these high plateaux that the golden plover and dunlin breed and in summer the air is filled with the sound of birdsong, mostly skylarks and pipits, with the occasional bubbling curlew and piping plover. In winter, this can be a sombre place with harsh gloomy weather, a few bedraggled sheep and a solitary foraging crow. But even then, a glimpse of a rare wintering bird can make an excursion memorable and in early spring the croaking hum of thousands of frogs collecting to mate in the bog pools can be an unforgettable sound.

The blanket bog merges into (relatively) drier moorland at lower altitudes where the peat is thinner and slopes steeper. Here the dominant vegetation varies with local factors and a complex pattern often emerges. Nevertheless certain types of moorland can be recognized. Heather moorland dominated by ling justly draws visitors in late summer when the slopes turn purple touched with splashes of vivid yellow from the late-flowering western gorse. Less popular are the adders with their distinctive zigzag pattern which frequent these drier moors. More often feared than seen, these will slip away at the first vibration of a footfall. Lizards are also common and can often be seen basking on a sunny rock or rustling away into the heather. The emperor moth with its distinctive caterpillar (fat, green and black with orange warts) feeds exclusively on heather as do red grouse which may be flushed whilst walking through heather or heard uttering their distinctive gutteral 'go-back' call.

Extensive heather moorland can be seen around the Warren House Inn/Hameldown area. Management to maintain it is essential. Burning and grazing are the tools used over centuries but both are double-edged. Frequent burning and intensive grazing can both destroy heather moorland within a few years, weakening the heather and thereby allowing other species to invade – often bracken on the drier soils and unpalatable purple moor grass on the wetter ones. On the other hand, without burning and grazing the heather moor would eventually turn into woodland as tree seedlings grow unchecked but not before old leggy heather had provided fuel for extensive and deep 'accidental' moorland fires, the effects of which could last for decades as in other uplands. Careful rotational burning and light grazing removes old leggy growth and stimulates new young shoots which will maintain this characteristic moorland habitat.

The British breeding population of dunlin is somewhere between 4000–8000 pairs. The Dartmoor population is only a very small part of this. However, here it occurs at the southern limit of the breeding range and is of great regional importance as Dartmoor is the only regular breeding site in southern England. On Dartmoor dunlin is found only on the most extensive unbroken tracts of blanket bog.

Generalised representation of woodland, moorland and blanket bog continuun. Prehistoric peoples cleared much of the natural woodland cover on high Dartmoor – accidentally by fires and deliberately for agricultural reasons – and in effect moorland has been 'inserted' between the blanket bogs and retreating woodland. The moorland resource has been used almost continuously through the centuries but climatic, ecological and human factors still influence moorland processes.

The true Dartmoor white-faced sheep have been largely displaced by northern mountain sheep like the Blackface (shown here) and Cheviot whose breeding ewes can spend the winter on the Moor.

Grass moorland is fairly common and can result from mismanagement of heather moorland. Two types of grass moorland can be distinguished – one dominated by bents and fescues and the other by purple moor grass. The former is of some use agriculturally and it is here that the largest numbers of sheep, cattle and ponies will be found. Other grass species include sweet vernal grass, heath grass, bristle bent, mat grass and red fescue. Sedges such as green-ribbed and pill sedge join more obvious 'herbs' – heath bedstraw, milkwort and tormentil – to create a grazed lawn studded with colour in the summer. These areas are not large in extent and often result from intensive grazing or trampling – good examples can be found around major car parks and picnic areas.

Purple moor grass will tolerate wetter soils (hence its dominance on the southern blanket bog) and has few other species associated with it. Its lush growth, particularly after burning, can produce

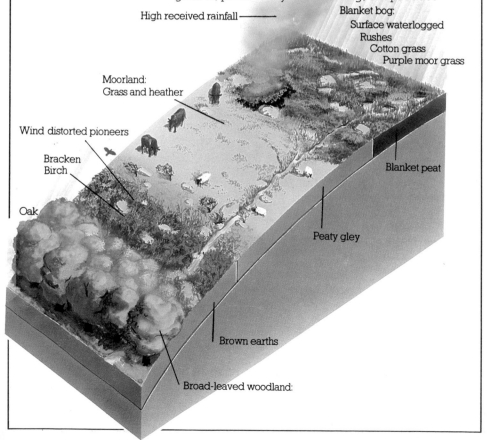

High received rainfall

Blanket bog:
Surface waterlogged
Rushes
Cotton grass
Purple moor grass

Moorland:
Grass and heather

Wind distorted pioneers

Bracken
Birch

Blanket peat

Oak

Peaty gley

Brown earths

Broad-leaved woodland:

some feed for stock in the spring (the main reason for burning it) but unless grazed evenly this growth soon becomes coarse and unpalatable producing large quantities of tussocky raffia which swamp any smaller plants. The only agricultural option then is to burn again to get rid of this growth and hence either an annual burning programme is necessary (with the inherent damage to wildlife and the ecosystem) or vast areas of monotonous moor grass will remain. Nevertheless these areas do have some value for wildlife providing cover for meadow pipits, skylarks, voles and foxes amongst others. The orangey-brown small heath butterfly can be abundant here during the summer months.

Whortleberry (bilberry) can be found in many areas of the moor, particularly on drier slopes. Until the early days of this century it was an annual late summer tradition for families from villages around the moor to go to good 'hurt' gathering areas to harvest the crop of purple berries.

The better grasses are often invaded by bracken which can cover extensive slopes with dense summer growth and winter litter. Bracken is generally believed to have spread in recent years on a world-wide scale and Dartmoor is no exception. Locally the spread may be assisted by too frequent burning (bracken has deep underground rhizomes unaffected by winter and spring fires and will not burn when green in summer) and by a reduction in the numbers of cattle which can trample it much more effectively than sheep. Over-grazing, which leaves the bracken intact but weakens other species, will also hasten its spread. It is valued for little other than its contribution to a rough landscape and is most attractive when dead. However bracken slopes do provide a major habitat for whinchats. Where hawthorn and rowan trees have managed to struggle through the bracken canopy these areas are also much used by tree pipits, yellowhammers and redstarts. Mammals such as foxes, badgers and rabbits will use bracken for cover and it is taken by both badgers and humans for bedding (the latter nowadays using it for stock during the winter).

The raven is frequently seen croaking over the open moor or seen barrelleling on thermals. A small number of moorland nest sites occur utilising appropriate trees and tor and quarry ledges.

Although bilberry or whortleberry is common throughout Dartmoor, there are a few areas where it forms an almost continuous carpet. These bilberry moors are found around the southern edges of the blanket bog, for instance on Brent Moor above Shipley Bridge. The young leaves in summer turn these moors bright yellow-green and the delicate red/pink bell-like flowers soon develop into blue-black berries.

Moorland vegetation types often merge into each other and are not defined on the ground by hard lines. Neither are they uniform and they are interrupted by tors and clitter, boulders and bogs

Saixcolous (growing on rocks) lichens encrust outcrops, moorstone, walls and buildings. On this granite boulder grow *Parmelia caperata* and, on the left, *Parmelia saxatilis*.

Moorland crowfoot, confined in the main to moorland waters in the west and north of the British Isles, flowers from May to September.

which in themselves form unique environments.

Tors can appear stark and lifeless but peer into any crevice and you will invariably see shade-tolerant ferns and mosses, slugs and spiders, lairs for sheep and fox, woodland plants or even a nest. The ledges will support moss and lichen gardens and plants such as greater woodrush, bilberry, heather or even bluebell enjoy the protection offered from grazing. Ravens, kestrels and occasionally buzzards will nest here. Shade and shelter are the most important ecological factors on tors and aspect has a noticeable influence. Compare for instance the west and east faces of tors, or the north and south faces. The flora can be entirely different reflecting prevailing weather conditions – this is particularly true of the lichens. Some rarer ferns also are associated with tors – Wilson's filmy fern and beech fern – as is fir clubmoss. Insects will often congregate around the top of tors, the most conspicuous perhaps being butterflies, such as painted ladies, on migration. But flies, wasps and flying ants will dance around tors in the summer.

The clitter which spreads below tors supports a similar flora and fauna depending on extent and aspect. It is here that many moorland foxes have their earths, foraging on the surrounding moorland by night although they can often be seen during the day. Rabbits inhabit clitter which must form a substitute for the 'buries' or warrens in which they were farmed for over 700 years. Wheatears, too, frequent these dry rocky places and can be seen flicking their white tail bards throughout the summer.

Isolated boulders can be important perching places; pellets and droppings often accumulate here. These in turn affect the lichen flora which colonizes these boulders, leading to an increase in nitrogen-loving lichens such as the bright yellow *Candelariella* species.

Valley bogs or mires are one of the most important open moorland habitats. Recognizable from a distance by their brighter green colour and, close up, their quaking surfaces ('featherbeds'), these bogs have accumulated peat over centuries by virtue of their position in valley bottoms or at a significant break of slope. Some of the biggest are at about 1,200 ft (365 m) where rivers and streams often slacken due to a change in gradient. Examples are at Foxtor Mires, Taw Marsh and on a smaller scale, Haytor and Blackslade Downs. Such bogs differ from the blanket bog in that instead of the wetness being solely rain derived, waterlogging here is also due to the slow through-flow of drainage water. This moving water has a relatively high availability of nutrients from the surrounding catchment and enables many plants to flourish which are not found elsewhere. In summer valley bogs are full of colour. Small and delicate plants such as bog pimpernel, ivy-leaved bellflower, pale butterwort and sundews (mostly *Drosera rotundifolia*) are dotted amongst lawns of bog mosses (sphagnum species) whilst larger plants such as bog bean and bog asphodel form dense stands where conditions are suitable. The bog mosses may continue to grow, building hummocks which will eventually lose contact with the groundwater. All their nutrients are then obtained from rainwater and these hummocks can become much more acid or nutrient-poor than the surrounding hollows which still contain a very diverse flora. Valley bogs with this hummock-hollow formation are amongst the best on Dartmoor and are very vulnerable to disturbance. Occasionally the hummocks may coalesce to form 'raised bogs' but today this only happens on Dartmoor on a small scale.

The buzzard is Dartmoor's largest bird of prey.

It is in these valley bogs that one finds some of the most interesting dragonflies. The keeled skimmer, four-spotted chaser, black darter and common hawker can all be found patrolling here, together with the large red and common blue damselfly. Curlew, lapwing, snipe and reed bunting will nest here; frogs congregate and are taken by herons, foxes and buzzards. These species and others like them link the open moorland habitats through their food chains and social dynamics in such a way that they cannot be isolated. All are essential to the health of the Dartmoor ecosystem.

The most extensive broad-leaved woodland within the national park is to be found clothing the steep valleys of the major rivers around the edge of the granite and where they leave the high moorland. The dramatic scenery of the wooded gorges in the Teign, Bovey, Dart, Walkham and East Okement river valleys has probably not changed drastically since the moorland above them was cleared by early man. This woodland is the direct successor to the original Dartmoor forest of 6,000 years ago. The tree species now are predominantly sessile oak with occasional hazel and rowan. Ash and sallow can be found in wet flush sites together with alder along the riverside, and locally on base-rich sites small-leaved lime is abundant. Wild

Tormentil, a small flower very common on short-cropped moorland swards, but which also colonizes medieval tinners' spoil-heaps.

Birchwood, Lustleigh.

service tree is thinly scattered in ancient woods on the eastern side of the park. There are indications even here, though, of the influence of man. Since the earliest times woodland products have been utilized. The multiple-stemmed oaks and even canopy we see today result from a long history of coppicing which only ceased recently. For centuries, seen from above, the woods would have presented a patchwork of small regular areas of different-aged coppice, mature standard trees and clear-felled areas. On newly coppiced areas woodmen might be stripping bark from the felled oaks and stacking it to dry (to be used eventually in the tanning industry) whilst charcoal burners built piles of heartwood (later to be fired) on small purpose-built circular platforms. Today the woods are quiet but a legacy of charcoal hearths, meandering paths and an almost pure oak canopy remain. Most valley woods are now unmanaged and this creates problems for their long-term future. With an ageing canopy and little oak regeneration beneath due to lack of light and, in some cases, grazing, these beautiful woods are in dire need of management.

However, their intrinsic ecological interest can, for the time being, still be enjoyed. The lushness and diversity of the ground flora depend to a large extent on the intensity of grazing. Ungrazed woods can have a thick carpet of bilberry on poorer soils as at Yarner Wood, bluebell or bramble as in the Wray Valley and a number of woodland herbs such as wood sorrel, wood sanicle, yellow archangel, honeysuckle, primrose, wood sage and wood spurge. Ferns are luxuriant, particularly on north-facing slopes, the commonest being broad buckler fern, scaly male fern, male fern, lady fern and hart's-tongue fern. The greatest number of species is to be found where the soils are richest – along valley bottoms, flush zones and on heavier soils.

Grazed woods have far fewer plants but the ground flora can be very rich in mosses, liverworts and lichens which benefit from the removal of the field layer. Mossy cushions may be made up of many different species and although lichens can be found amongst these mosses, the most impressive growth clothes the branches above. The trunks of mature trees near river courses often support a rich and unusual lichen flora reflecting air purity and continuity of woodland habitat.

Mosses and lichens grow prolifically in the damp and unpolluted atmosphere of Dartmoor.

Broad-leaved valley woods are also the summer stronghold of birds such as the pied flycatcher, wood warbler and redstart. Woodpeckers, nuthatch, buzzards and tits are common and woodcock may be flushed in winter. Deer may occasionally be seen, particularly roe deer. Although parties of red deer are known to move through Dartmoor woods, they are much less common than on Exmoor. Badger setts are most frequently found in woodland and can reach an enormous size, often being centuries old. Badger numbers are still very high, particularly on the moorland fringe, though they will range, and even live, miles out on the open moor. The ubiquitous fox is at home here as are grey squirrels.

Signs of dormice, wood mice, voles, moles and hedgehogs may all be encountered in a woodland walk and during the summer months woodland butterflies are noticeable. Speckled woods locked in a spiralling fight in a sunny woodland glade, white admirals feeding on brambles, strong-flying silver-washed fritillaries and purple hairstreaks flitting amongst the canopy are all part of the summer woodland scene.

Other broad-leaved woods include the three small upland oak copses – Black Tor Copse, Piles Copse and Wistmans Wood – the last renowned for its romantic, gnarled appearance. All are found above 900 ft (275 m) on the west-facing, clittery sides of steep valleys surrounded by open moorland, and all are dominated by pedunculate oak. Their history has been the subject of much ecological speculation. The most likely explanation is that these woods are also remnants of the original forest cover which have survived in modified form for various reasons in sites on granite soils which can be tolerated better by pendunculate oak than by sessile oak. Today, they are heavily grazed but full of epiphytic lichens and ferns, mosses, gnarled trees and a mysterious , wild atmosphere.

Modern foresters have until recently, concentrated their attentions on conifer plantations as a source of reliable, productive timber. Dartmoor has its share of these; Bellever, Soussons and Fernworthy Forest are the largest and were mostly planted in the 1920s. They are dominated by Norway and Sitka spruce and have created a very different habitat to the open moorland they replaced. Few plants grow under the dense shade once the canopy begins to close, but along rides and in other open places the original moorland flora survives.

Moorland grasses, tormentil and heath bedstraw will be found growing with heather – usually ling and cross-leaved heath. The rare Dorset heath survives at 1,250 ft (380 m) in a clearing at Soussons Forest, having been introduced earlier this century.

These areas can also contain lizards and adders, badgers, foxes, stoats, voles and shrews and grey squirrels are common.

Crossbills and siskins have both benefited from

Black Tor Copse, West Okement Valley, the northernmost of the three primeval oak groves of high Dartmoor. Here between 1,200 and 1,530ft (336m and 467m) above sea level grow Devon's highest altitude oaks.

the planting of conifers, as have goldcrests, whilst redpolls will nest in the early thicket stages. As the forests came into full production the proportion of clear-felled open areas and thicket stages has increased and they will become more valuable for plants and animals.

From the edge of open moorland to the national park boundary the landscape is basically one of enclosed farmland. In spite of, and in many cases, because of, a long history of intense human activity, this area provides unique habitats. Devon hedgebanks are justly famous for their early spring flowers but although the primroses and violets are certainly beautiful, it is as an all-year-round linear habitat that such hedgebanks are most ecologically valuable. Song birds, such as dunnock, song thrush, blackbird and robin, nest in their dense tangle, feed on their berries and seek shelter during winter storms. They will in turn be hunted by sparrowhawk swooping low over the hedge in surprise attack. Small mammals, mice, voles, shrews and weasels join hedgehog, fox and badger in using the hedge both as a foraging base and as a source of food and shelter.

Many Dartmoor hedgebanks are hundreds of years old and have developed a rich and varied flora. Ash, oak, hazel, field maple, hawthorn, blackthorn and holly may all be found in a 30yd (10m) stretch. Rarer species such as small-leaved lime and wild service tree occur in hedges on the eastern fringes of the park. Here marjoram and columbine grow with more typical hedge plants such as shining cranesbill, jack-by-the-hedge, greater stitchwort and the ubiquitous primroses and violets.

Stone walls too provide habitat. Especially where earth is used in their construction, small plants such as English stonecrop and wall pepper will grow with hawkweeds, navelwort and sheep's bit to provide a summer rock garden of colour.

All these flowers provide food for many insects and butterflies seen in summer months along the many 'green lanes' traversed by footpaths and bridlepaths. Butterflies find shelter here – particularly meadow brown, ringlet, speckled wood and the pearl-bordered and silver-washed fritillaries.

Some fields may never have been ploughed because they are too wet or too rocky or they may have reverted to 'roughland' after an earlier period of agricultural expansion. Such areas are often free

The pearl-bordered fritillary emerges early – in April – and feeds on violets. During the last 100 years all our woodland fritillaries have suffered a severe contraction of range because of the decline in traditional woodland management practices; management such as coppicing provided glades in which their food plants grew. However, in the south west, suitable habitats still exist and numbers of such butterflies are quite high.

The ivy-leaved bellflower favours a mild Atlantic climate and thrives in valley bogs, flushes and often on the sides of small moorland streams; Dartmoor is its national stronghold.

from disturbance for most of the year and can be havens for wildlife. Wet rough grassland fills many valley bottoms and is often used as summer grazing for bullocks. Here many orchids flourish (mostly southern marsh orchid and heath spotted orchid) along with rushes, sedges and coarse grasses. Wet areas may have a typical range of bog plants including pale butterwort, ivy-leaved bellflower and bog mosses. Petty whin, marsh plume thistle, bog myrtle and creeping willow can occasionally be found. Breeding butterflies can include the nationally declining marsh fritillary and the marbled white which is more usually associated with lowland areas. These rough wet fields also provide important cover for wintering wildfowl – snipe and woodcock – and larger mammals.

Dry, rough, rocky areas are less interesting botanically – they tend to be dominated by bracken – but they also provide cover, shelter and nest sites for birds and mammals.

Traditional haymeadows which have never been ploughed, or had artifical fertilizers or pesticides applied to them, are unfortunately rare on Dartmoor as elsewhere. However, they have survived in a few places either because their herb-rich hay is valued or by chance. These meadows are beautiful in early summer. Yellow hawkweed, purple knapweed, white ox-eye daisy, and blue scabious wave above a carpet of bird's-foot trefoil, eyebright and speedwell scattered with greater butterfly orchids. Sweet-smelling grasses and fluttering butterflies (mostly blues, whites and browns) complete the picture. Sadly, such meadows are disappearing. Silage-making is a safer alternative in an unpredictable climate and favours new, fast-growing grasses, which in turn need heavy doses of artificial fertilizer.

Small woods and ponds add variety and interest to a farmland landscape where animals, plants and people have co-existed for centuries.

Flowing from the high moor, past tors and clitter, through bogs, woodland and farmland, rivers link these habitats and provide important wildlife corridors. They also provide attractive picnic sites and riverside walks and being so narrow are vulnerable to human disturbance.

Nevertheless even the shy Dartmoor otter may pass through tangled valleys in enclosed farmland, up through steep, wooded gorges and on to the open moor where riverside boulders and shrubby islands will be used for cover. Crossing

watersheds, the otter may descend through another
river system to a north or south Devon estuary.

Otters unfortunately are much less common than
formerly (mainly due to pesticide use in the 1950s
and 60s) and although signs may be found mink are
more likely to be seen by the walker. Escaping from

a fur farm near Moretonhampstead in the 1950s and
first breeding on the upper reaches of the Teign,
mink spread eventually to all Devon rivers and
beyond. These admittedly handsome creatures will
take birds, rabbits, voles, rats, poultry and even
kittens and puppies as well as fish but their true
impact on native fauna, particularly otters, is not
known.

The Dartmoor rivers, being unpolluted, support
populations of salmon, trout and grayling. In spring
or autumn, salmon leaping up the weirs across
rivers like the Dart and Teign on their way to the
spawning beds can be a dramatic sight particularly
if the river is in spate. The bigger weirs are
equipped with special fish passes but even so it can
be a struggle and the strength and determination of
the salmon is impressive.

Birds will also use the rivers as corridors –
dippers, herons and cormorants may be seen
passing up and downstream whilst the grey wagtail
remains more local, flicking its tail amongst the
riverside boulders. Both dippers and grey wagtails
feed on water insects; whilst dippers will walk
under swift water to take the larvae of dragonfly,
caddisfly and mayfly, the grey wagtail snaps at the

The otter, a mammal that
has greatly declined in
numbers in Britain over
recent years but still may
be occasionally sighted
on the major Dartmoor
rivers.

River Meavy. Below their
moorland tracts Dartmoor
river valleys provide
completely contrasting
wildlife habitats.

adults a few feet above the water surface.

Riverside plants both reflect and contribute to the
habitat through which the river is passing. Lemon-
scented fern can be found high up on the East Dart
growing alongside heather and purple moor grass.
Further down, royal fern fronds can reach a height
of over 6 ft (2 m) along wooded banks and the tiny
Tunbridge filmy fern grows under shaded riverside
rocks. Rivers act as corridors for plants too,
effectively aiding dispersal for many species. Plant
species can thereby spread rapidly through a river
system.

Foreign invaders, with few native pests to impede
their progress, illustrate this. Himalayan balsam or
policeman's helmet was first recorded in Devon in
1888 and has since spread to grow in luxuriant
stands beside many rivers, notably the Teign,
Bovey and Dart. Pink purslane, a native of North
America, was first recorded from Haytor Vale in
1923 and its pretty, bright pink, star-like flowers can
now be found along most watercourses on
Dartmoor.

Vigorous native species can also spread rapidly
along rivers. Hemlock water dropwort will form
dense stands over 6 ft (2 m) tall alongside streams

Fernworthy Forest and Reservoir – a man-made landscape of the twentieth century, already a wildlife haven, and an area valued for quiet recreation.

and rivers and can be a problem to farmers if growing in cattle pastures. It is highly poisonous, particularly the roots, and cattle are often killed by eating plants newly cleared from choked streams.

Slow-moving waters can have a rather different flora. Leats, particularly if not regularly maintained, can become full of pondweed and water crowfoot. As these trap sediment and mud accumulates, the flora resembles that of a valley bog with bog bean, bog mosses and rushes. These leats can be important for dragonfly larvae, and the adults can often be seen patrolling up and down them.

Reservoirs tend to have few plants associated with their margins. Fluctuating water levels make colonization difficult although the bright green shore-weed carpets the draw-down zone (between high and low water) around the older reservoirs, for example at Hennock. Wintering wildfowl however make good use of these areas and goosander, teal, pochard and tufted duck may be seen with resident Canada geese and mallard. The reservoirs are stocked with fish, much appreciated by local cormorants and herons.

Dartmoor is a dynamic landscape inhabited by many plants and animals including humans, all inexorably linked and dependent on each other for their continued survival. This is the total ecological resource which is and will continue to be so fascinating for visitors and residents alike.

8 **Dartmoor today and tomorrow**

A sense of social cohesion is strong in the communities on and around the hills of Dartmoor. The relative isolation of the farms, hamlets and villages tends to foster a neighbourly interest and concern and a willingness to participate in social activities, of which there are many throughout the year.

Summer is the time for fêtes and carnivals. Every village has its day, and the bigger ones will have two. Moretonhampstead and Okehampton, for example, have an agricultural-type show on one day and a carnival on another. The larger shows tend to have a strong agricultural element, sometimes having their own speciality (goats at Lustleigh, sheep at Moretonhampstead) and all the towns and villages have flower shows at some time.

One Dartmoor village day that has won international fame is Widecombe Fair. Thousands of people come to what is increasingly a commercial fair, although it used to be a general agricultural show. The quiet East Webburn Valley is transformed into something looking more like an ant nest when seen from the top of Widecombe Hill.

Outdoor sport on Dartmoor tends to be much the same as in any rural area. Riding has always been a favourite pastime and hunting was particularly popular before the First World War. Fishing along the main Dartmoor rivers has always been popular although trout and salmon are not as plentiful as they used to be because of marine pollution.

The church is still an important part of village and parish life. Some changes have inevitably occurred and nowadays the clergy tend to look after several parishes.

Those villages which still have primary schools (surprisingly numerous with twenty-five or so within and adjacent to the national park) benefit by the vitality and interest that the schools contribute to local life. A few villages (North Bovey and Lustleigh, for example) lost their schools in the 1950s and '60s, with pupils having to be bussed to nearby schools – a practice which is far more widespread for secondary students since there are only four comprehensive schools around Dartmoor.

Special signposted routes have been provided to ease the burden of tourist traffic on Dartmoor's roads and lanes.

As in other parts of Britain, public transport on Dartmoor has declined a lot over the past few decades. Three railway lines used to serve Dartmoor: Tavistock to Okehampton, and the Yelverton to Princetown and Moretonhampstead branches. These were all closed by the early 1960s. Now it is the rural bus which is becoming scarce; although the routes still exist, fewer buses run and seldom after six o'clock. Some villages have a private minibus service once a week on market day and during the summer the National Park Authority sponsors a bus across the Moor from Plymouth to Exeter, via Moretonhampstead.

With increased use of the private car, some village shops have become less important for those people who are able to travel to the larger towns. Nevertheless, village food shops, post offices, chemists and ironmongers are generally well supported, particularly when seen in the context of their general decline in other parts of rural Britain.

This is Dartmoor today, a vital part of rural Britain in which the National Park Authority plays a key role. The park's statutory objectives, laid down in the National Parks and Access to the Countryside Act 1949, are to conserve and enhance the quality of the landscape, and to promote public enjoyment of that landscape.

Since the 1968 Countryside Act, and more particularly the Sandford Committee recommendations partly accepted by government in 1976, the social and economic well being of local communities within the park is also an object of policy (though still not a statutory responsibility).

Rock climbing, Haytor Rocks.

Parke, Bovey Tracey, a National Trust property, the headquarters of the Dartmoor National Park Authority.

Since 1951, Devon County Council (as the National Park Authority) has delegated the responsibility for carrying out the objectives of the national park to a Dartmoor National Park Committee; two-thirds of the National Park Committee are representatives of the county council and relevant district councils, while one-third is appointed by the Secretary of State for the Environment. In 1974 (after the Local Government Act 1972) Dartmoor was given a National Park Officer and the supporting staff necessary to create a working organization. Based at Parke, Bovey Tracey (just outside the national park boundary), the national park employs around fifty full-time staff, whose work in carrying out national park policy is funded largely by the Department of the Environment through the National Park Supplementary Grant (seventy-five per cent) as well as through the Rate Support Grant (sixteen per cent) and by Devon ratepayers (nine per cent). In addition, the authority generates a certain amount of income from the sale of publications and from fees for planning applications and the like.

In pursuance of its two statutory objectives, the National Park Authority is the local planning authority, taking into account national, county, and its own local policies. It is also charged with producing a National Park Plan in which it sets out positive management and planning objectives. The County Structure Plan concentrates economic development in six Selected Local Centres (Ashburton, Buckfastleigh, South Brent, Yelverton/Horrabridge, Chagford and Moretonhampstead).

The Authority is involved in agricultural development as a result of the grant notification scheme, whereby a farmer intending to carry out work on the farm for which a Ministry of Agriculture, Fisheries, and Food grant is to be claimed has to give notice to the Authority. If the Authority does not approve of the proposal, it can negotiate a management agreement which may involve paying the farmer compensation. If this cannot be agreed, then MAFF must decide whether it will pay the grant before the work starts.

To provide a demonstration of conservation principles in action, the National Park Authority has acquired some open moorland at Holne Moor and Haytor, together with some woodland at Wray Cleave, Casely Wood, Sanduck Wood and Whiddon Scrubs. These are managed by a team of conservation, archaeology, and recreation specialists, who also advise farmers and other landowners in the park on landscape matters.

To disseminate the national park purposes as widely as possible among visitors and local inhabitants alike, the Authority operates a Ranger and Information Service. There are now nine full-time Rangers, each with a different area to look after. They undertake all kinds of practical work, from advising visitors and collecting litter to helping with swaling, mending walls and planting trees. The Information Service has Information Centres at Newbridge, Steps Bridge, Postbridge, Princetown, Tavistock, Okehampton and Bovey Tracey. An annual broadsheet is produced – *The Dartmoor Visitor* – as well as other publications on various aspects of the Moor. There is a programme of guided walks, particularly in the visitor season, and an Education Ranger helps teachers and youth groups plan their visits to the park. The Authority stresses the importance of education in its 1983 Plan Review.

Postbridge National Park Information Centre.

What about the Dartmoor over which this National Park Authority watches? Conflicts inevitably arise in the outstanding landscape. The recent controversial decision to route the A30 Okehampton bypass south of the town, through part of Dartmoor instead of adopting the northern alternative, suggests both the way things might have gone generally over the last thirty years if there had been no national park and at the same time the shortcomings of the present system.

Dartmoor's modern appearance is the result of human occupation of a terrain whose intractability has in the past preserved a balance between human and non-human elements. But technological developments in the present century, combined with the increasing size and capital resources of the organizations who use them, have given humans the power to destroy that balance. The brake on extreme change that was once applied by the granite, the peat and the altitude, now has its lever lodged in the hands of the National Park Authority, who pulls on it only to discover it does not control certain big wheels driven from outside.

Dartmoor has been used as a military training ground since 1870. The amount of land occupied reached its peak at the end of the Second World War, but even though it has now been reduced by about half, the area still stands at some 33,000 acres and there are no signs of any further reduction in the future. Training takes place principally in the north-west quarter of the Moor – the highest tor, Yes Tor, where it is still the custom for people to watch the sun rise on Easter Sunday in the hope of seeing the device of a lamb in the disc, has two military huts built on it. A large compound has grown up on moorland at Okehampton Camp, and a tarmac road for military vehicles penetrates a third of the way towards the centre of the northern plateau. Practice with live ammunition is involved; on days when there is firing, the public is warned to stay away by red flags flown from permanent flagstaffs erected on tors.

The live ammunition is bound to disturb wildlife – much of the firing area is designated as a Site of Special Scientific Interest – and damage to archaeological sites and terrain has taken place. Moreover there is always the distinct danger of an accident involving people. The National Park Authority's position, agreed by the Government, is that military use is incompatible with the idea of Dartmoor as a national park, but in practice it is not able to do any more than negotiate small concessions such as the reduction of firing during peak visitor periods. The Ministry of Defence has a

Meldon Reservoir sits in a dramatic stretch of the West Okement Valley. It was completed in 1972 and was the last to be built on Dartmoor.

999 year lease on Okehampton Camp which expires in 2891, and it owns the freehold of the Willworthy Range – about a quarter of the total area.

In a sense, though, the military presence on Dartmoor injects, by the starkest possible means, realism into idealistic notions that a national park can be free from the contradictions in thought and the conflicts of interest that bedevil the conservation of the rest of the country. Because the local economy is depressed, the military presence is regarded by many as vital to it (though the economy could be boosted by other means). More problematically, few have ever felt entirely happy with suggestions that other areas such as Salisbury Plain and Scotland could readily accommodate the training which now takes place on Dartmoor.

Dartmoor now has eight reservoirs, two of them built since it became a national park, providing two-thirds of Devon's water. Large areas of water are not part of Dartmoor's natural legacy, and the valleys they have drowned contained much that was of interest topographically, archaeologically and ecologically. When a reservoir was proposed for the head of the Swincombe River in the 1960s, opposition from the National Park Authority and notably the Dartmoor Preservation Association headed by Lady Sylvia Sayer resulted in the scheme being turned down by Parliament. A different kind of reservoir is now to be built at Roadford, outside the boundary of the park, which will do more than the Swincombe proposal could ever have done. The National Park Authority's position is that no more moorland valleys should be flooded. It is true that reservoirs near sources of streams and rivers are often poor storage arrangements – the lower down the system, the better the reservoir.

Someone, however, is entitled to ask: if a reservoir within the national park is such a bad thing, why should it be built at Roadford? It is only if reservoirs in themselves come to be regarded as an inappropriate solution to the water-shortage dilemma that this problem will disappear.

While the National Park Authority has been unable to resist the developments so far referred to, it has acted to prevent the spread of housing development outside villages and to preserve the look of old buildings, except in the case of buildings related to agricultural requirements (over which it has little control). But planning control itself is not directly related to the promotion of thriving upland communities, in which housing plays a crucial part.

Ponsworthy. Sympathetic renovation has taken place in keeping with the traditional building style of the area.

A conserved environment has encouraged second-home ownership and the conversion of ordinary rented accommodation to holiday accommodation, thereby reducing the stock of housing for local needs. At an auction in the parish of Widecombe not so long ago, a massive cheer went up from local people present when the property in question went to a local bidder, indicating both the increasing rarity of this outcome and the strength of feeling on the subject among Dartmoor residents.

Too much adherence to the styles of the past in the building that is permitted has not necessarily helped to foster new cultural ideas which are vital for the life and self-respect of a healthy community. The publication of a booklet *Building in the Dartmoor National Park* setting out positive guidelines for building with local materials and with local styles in mind has gone some way towards encouraging the integration of old and new.

However, as things stand, young people are often forced to move out of the area as much through lack of accommodation as poor employment opportunities. Such compulsory mobility on a large scale destroys the individualism and continuity of community cultures, and is likely to contribute to social problems. One way forward lies in the encouragement of housing co-operatives and housing associations, which the National Park Authority has assisted, and whose initiation it discusses with other parties. The problem is a national one and requires a national solution.

It is true that changes in farming practice and an increase in conifer afforestation have had unforseen consequences for the conservation of the national parks, and Dartmoor is no exception. However the most damaging effects cannot be laid at the door of the small landowner or tenant farmer, but are the responsibility of the two large organizations who have given the lead. In its drive to increase productivity and efficiency, MAFF has until recently encouraged land improvement and intensification of cultivation and stock-keeping regardless of the particular environment in which the farm operates. The situation was further compounded by EEC grants for Less Favoured Areas.

The Duchy of Cornwall began afforestation, notably after the First World War, at Beardown and Brimpts, and as time went on Fernworthy, Bellever and Soussons became the major plantations taken over by the Forestry Commission. Planting had also begun in the catchment areas of the Burrator and Hennock Reservoirs, and shelterbelts had become a new part of the scene in the East Dart Valley. Private plantings had taken place meanwhile in the lower Dart Valley at Ausewell and Buckland.

At first, the Forestry Commission pursued a single-minded policy of planting quick-rotation conifers that has percolated through to small landowners on the Moor wishing to turn some of their land over to trees. The Forestry Commission also paid grants to farmers for plantations aimed at timber production, which in effect meant planting conifers.

Over the last few years, however, both MAFF and the Forestry Commission have adopted a more positive attitude towards conservation. MAFF now pays grants for activities such as wall-building and hedging, while the Forestry Commission operates a Broad-leaved Woodland Grant Scheme specifically aimed at encouraging the maintenance of existing broad-leaved woodlands and the creation of new ones. This is a welcome development, but farmers and other landowners who have long been educated in the past policies of these organizations cannot be expected to change direction very quickly.

It is perhaps in these two fields that some of the best work of the National Park Authority is currently being done – not by legislation but by positive example, encouragement and advice. Ann and Malcolm MacEwen, in their book *National Parks: Conservation or Cosmetics?* have argued the case for a low-input/low-output type of agriculture in the uplands. A wealth of information on traditional hill-farming practices exists in the minds of some of the

The agricultural grant notification scheme has led to a closer working relationship between the farming community and the National Park Authority.

In the last century and the first quarter of this most cattle kept on Dartmoor 'in-country' farms were South Devons. It is the largest breed of cattle native to Britain. They were ideal animals for the traditional mixed farm – a dual purpose beast valued for its meat and good milk yields. Having given way to pure dairy and beef breeds in the last fifty years, it is again becoming favoured by many farmers.

older inhabitants of Dartmoor and combined with new ecological information it could form the basis for such low-input/low-output farming. Organic growing and stock-rearing are already practised in some places on the Moor; the market for 'pure' produce is one of the few farming markets likely to increase in the immediate future, and Dartmoor might be particularly suitable for the production of 'pure' meat. The growing animal welfare movement points in this direction too.

Low-input implies the return to a degree of self-sufficiency; the practice of traditional forms of farm woodland management such as hedgelaying and coppicing of small areas of broad-leaved trees can help in this by supplying home demand for firewood, durable fencing stakes (oak and chestnut) and timber. With new methods of processing, such as small portable saw-mills, the production of saw-timber from mature broad-leaved trees for use on the farm where they grew is becoming more feasible.

The Dartmoor Commons Act of 1985 is aimed at securing the future of Dartmoor's common land as a vital part of traditional Dartmoor farming. It was promoted by the National Park Authority in

association with the Commoners' Association, and it is a unique Act in that it addresses itself to the problem of management of the commons and is not just confined to the question of access. It legalizes public access to nearly all parts of the common land in the national park and at the same time makes provision for the setting up of byelaws to regulate public behaviour. The rest of the Act is concerned with the proper use of the commons by commoners. It made provision for the setting up of a Commoners' Council which has representatives from the commoners themselves (the majority), the National Park, the Duchy of Cornwall, other common landowners, and a vet. The Council is concerned with controlling livestock numbers on the commons, heather burning, bracken clearance, winter feeding and other matters related to the health of the moorland vegetation and the stock grazing on it.

Many of the farms abutting the Forest and other blocks of common land – as we have seen earlier – have newtakes of moorland, most of them stockproof. They are to the hill farmer the only moorland for his exclusive use – the rough grazing he can conserve at will, use for bulling heifers, or to ensure that only *his* rams serve *his* ewes. The importance of all this to his seasonal timetable, and the health and quality of his stock – especially lambs and calves – cannot be overstated. Newtakes in the late twentieth century therefore are very valuable and jealously protected by the good stockman. They also stand between the roads – and attendant car parks and the open moor of the plateau to which the visitor has a right of access under the Dartmoor

The Dartmoor Commons Act, 1985, seeks to secure the agricultural, landscape and recreation value of Dartmoor common land for the future.

Traditionalism, a vital component of twentieth-century Dartmoor life.

Commons Act. Some have rights of way through them – not always on the best lines from either the farmer's or the walker's points of view – some do not. The National Park Authority and the Duchy of Cornwall are inching towards reconciliation of the optimum value to the farmer and optimum experience of this enclosed moorland for the visitor.

The Dartmoor National Park Authority's fostering of the Devon Rural Skills Trust (DRST), its concern with common land, and its advocacy of both the planting and the management of broad-leaved trees (including a free tree scheme), is helping to prepare the ground for the lowering of capital input on Dartmoor farms, and just possibly an increase in labour.

Fortunately, Dartmoor does not pursue these activities merely as traditions in isolation from the rest of the country – the DRST operates throughout the county, and so avoids the risk that its way of life will come to be seen by visitors as a relic of the past, interesting as a museum piece, but largely irrelevant to their modern existence. Low-input farming must also be put forward as a hard-nosed form of progress, not as a cushioned means of preservation. In order for farmers to maintain their professional pride, farming must be a viable activity in market terms, not simply a subsidized showpiece. Likewise small-scale industry, using some modern equipment but avoiding pollution, has to be regarded as a form of conservation, because it enhances the human community that is the most vital link in the ecological web of the landscape.

Small-scale industry is encouraged both by the National Park Authority and by the Duchy of Cornwall, which is the biggest landowner on Dartmoor. The National Park Authority has worked closely with CoSIRA (the Council for Small Industries in Rural Areas) on factory projects in Moretonhampstead and Buckfastleigh, and looks favourably on proposals to convert redundant farm buildings to workshops. The Duchy has set up workshops at Powder Mills and at Princetown. The present industry on Dartmoor represents only a drop in the ocean by comparison with the part it played in former times. For example in 1850 *White's Directory of Devon* records Chagford as having eight shoemakers – it now has none, although shoemaking on the nineteenth-century small scale is showing signs of development in south Devon.

Farming is the backbone of the moorland economy and way of life but variety in the community around it is also important. From new-look village shops, such as one at Ilsington which sells local organic produce, to Sam Harris's scrapyard at Lettaford progress towards the integration of technology and nature is going on at ground level, and could profitably be further encouraged.

It is this integrated face which Dartmoor must hope to put forward to the eight million visitors who come annually. While tourism undoubtedly provides seasonal employment and welcome additional income for a number of Dartmoor residents, the conservation priorities of a national park and tourism's seasonal nature mean that it is unlikely to become the primary part of a thriving

The church of St Michael de Rupe on Brent Tor. This is one of the country's smallest churches yet one of the most prominent; it stands on an eroded volcanic cone, 1,100ft (335m) above sea level.

moorland economy. It also brings its share of problems – litter, traffic jams, disturbance and erosion are the minor ones – but potentially its worst effect is to undermine through commercialization communities which are exposed to it, thereby destroying, among other things, what the visitors come to see.

This can only be countered in the long run, like so much else in conservation, not by legislation, but by a change of attitude, a recognition that Dartmoor has a modern, if different, life of its own. The idea that Dartmoor is a place to get enjoyment out of without having to put anything back is as short-sighted as cutting down a wood without replanting it. Human attitudes are as much part of Dartmoor's ecology as the jays which help the regeneration of its ancient oakwoods by burying acorns.

Only if visitors come with the respect to enable them to learn from its example and apply the inspiration it provides to their own back gardens, will the cultural conditions prevail for places such as Dartmoor to survive as living and vital parts of modern society, safeguarded from the whims of central government by public opinion. Like the respect of the people in the past who built the chambered tombs, the stone rows and circles, the cairns, the churches and the chapels, this respect in the last analysis has to be a spiritual one. If the natural architecture of Brent Tor was to be crowned by human building, the only appropriate form for it to take was a house of worship.

Selected places of interest

The numbers after each place-name are the map grid references to help readers locate the places mentioned. Ordnance Survey maps include instructions on the use of these grid references.

ASHBURTON (SX 755695) Market town, formerly a stannary town, taking its name from the River Ashburn which runs through it. Important centre in the past for wool as well as tin. Dartmoor National Park's largest town. It has many buildings of historic and architectural interest.

BELSTONE (SX 619936) Overlooking the River Taw, this village lies on the edge of the open moor. Good access for walking on the northern moor. Village stocks. Irishman's Wall (SX 615919) is a seemingly purposeless wall on Belstone Common, intended as a newtake boundary but never finished.

BOVEY TRACEY (SX 815785) Market town just outside the national park boundary. The headquarters of the Dartmoor National Park Authority are here at Parke (SX 805786), on the road to Haytor. Information Centre in the town (run by the Chamber of Trade) and at Parke. National Nature Reserve at Yarner (SX 780785).

BRIDFORD (SX 816865) Small village on a hill above the Teign Valley. The granite church is notable for its beautiful sixteenth-century rood-screen.

BUCKFAST AND BUCKFASTLEIGH (SX 740661) The demolished Cistercian abbey at Buckfast was rebuilt by French Benedictine monks in the early part of this century and stands beside the River Dart. Buckfastleigh, a market town, was once dominated by the wool industry; a mill is still in operation. Underground limestone caves (Pengelley Caves Centre).

CHAGFORD (SX 701876) Small market town, formerly a stannary town. Something of an enigma, having maintained itself as a busy centre in spite of being isolated from major transport routes. Scorhill prehistoric stone circle on nearby Gidleigh Common (SX 654875).

DREWSTEIGNTON (SX 737909) Village set above the Teign Gorge. Fingle Bridge below is a good example of a late medieval packhorse bridge. Nearby is Spinsters' Rock (SX 700908), a prehistoric chambered tomb with its stones still standing, and so too one of the most recent of Dartmoor's 'monuments', Castle Drogo (SX 723902) built in granite this century by the architect Lutyens, now owned by the National Trust.

HOLNE (SX 706696) Village set above the Dart Gorge. The Dartmoor National Park Authority owns land at Holne Moor, including oak woodland. Holne Moor is the site of recent archaeological excavations of both prehistoric and medieval settlements.

LEE MOOR (SX 572618) Mining village just outside the national park boundary. Area of extensive china-clay workings. Nearby, Shaugh Moor – the site of important recent archaeological excavations of prehistoric settlement.

LYDFORD (SX 510847) Village which was once an important Saxon and Norman town, as well as once being the centre of the Dartmoor stannary administration. Well preserved Saxon and Norman remains, including the castle (a Norman keep). Lydford Gorge (National Trust).

MANATON (SX 750813) Village set above the Bovey Valley in some of Dartmoor's most thickly wooded country. Close by are Houndtor medieval village (SX 744788) and the prehistoric settlement at Grimspound (SX 701809). To the south lies Bowerman's Nose (SX 7428805), a large granite stack which has been petrified into a humanlike appearance. Becka Falls (SX 761801).

MARY TAVY (SX 505795) Sister village to Peter Tavy. Several abandoned mines in the area where copper, lead and tin mined. Wheal Betsy (SX 512813), owned by the National Trust, is the best surviving engine house on Dartmoor.

MERRIVALE (SX 548752) Small hamlet in the River Walkham Valley centred around the granite quarry which still operates. Nearby is a prehistoric sanctuary (SX 555747) with stone rows, circles, cairns and standing stones.

MORETONHAMPSTEAD (SX 754860) Market town. Almshouses date to the seventeenth century. Annual craft fair. Several prehistoric forts in the area including Cranbrook Castle (SX 738890) overlooking the Teign Gorge.

NEWBRIDGE (SX 711708) Fifteenth-century packhorse bridge over the River Dart, part of a series of bridges (Holne, Dartmeet, Two Bridges and Merrivale) which enabled the present route from south-east Dartmoor to Tavistock to replace other routes on higher ground. National Park Information Centre here.

OKEHAMPTON (SX 587952) Market town just outside the national park boundary but very much a 'moorland town'. National Park Information Centre here. Nearby is Okehampton Castle, now in ruins, parts of which date to eleventh century. Moorland rivers stretch above to Yes Tor and High Willhays, west of which lies Black Tor Beare (SX 566890), an ancient oakwood.

POSTBRIDGE (SX 647789) Village in the middle of Dartmoor on the East Dart River. It has been described as the 'prehistoric metropolis' of Dartmoor because of the many prehistoric remains in the vicinity. Site of the finest Dartmoor clapper bridge. National Park Information Centre. Youth Hostel at Bellever (SX 655774).

PRINCETOWN (SX 588735) Dartmoor's highest village. Visited primarily because of its famed prison which was built for French and American prisoners in 1806. It closed in 1815 but reopened as a convict prison in 1850. National Park Information Centre. South east is Whiteworks (SX 613710), the site of extensive nineteenth-century tin mining.

SHEEPSTOR (SX 560677) Village under the dominating tor from which it takes its name. Nearby is Burrator Reservoir, the first moorland reservoir to be built on Dartmoor. An area of great archaeological interest including prehistoric remains and at Ditsworthy (SX 584662) an abandoned warren house.

SOUTH ZEAL (SX 652935) The modern plan of the village preserves the layout of a medieval town, with the narrow strip fields of individual 'burgage plots' still visible north and south of the main street.

STEPS BRIDGE (SX 804883) Old bridge over the River Teign near Dunsford, set in the extensive oak woodland of the Teign Gorge. Devon Trust for Nature Conservation reserve and National Trust woodland with trails. National Park Information Centre. Youth Hostel.

TAVISTOCK (SX 483745) Large market town on the River Tavy lying to the west of Dartmoor, but connected to it throughout its history. The site of a very powerful Benedictine abbey which dominated the area before its dissolution. Formerly a stannary town and the centre of the nineteenth-century copper-mining boom. National Park Information Centre in Bedford Square. A few miles to the south west is Morwellham (SX 445696), an industrial museum based on the copper mines and riverside quay.

TWO BRIDGES (SX 609750) The confluence of the Cowsic River and the West Dart River where the two trans-Dartmoor roads intersect. Up the West Dart River lies the ancient oakwood of Wistman's Wood (SX 613773).

WIDECOME IN THE MOOR (SX 719768) Village famous for its fair held on the second Tuesday in September, but also possessing a fine church, the so-called 'cathedral of the moor', with a remarkable tower, a testimony to the wealth which the tin trade brought to the area.

Glossary

ash house – circular building once used for storing ash, confined to an area of East Dartmoor

beam – as part of a place-name, it indicates the site of former open-cast tin workings.

beehive hut – a cache usually with a domed roof, once covered with turves, for tools and ingots constructed by medieval tinners

beare – wood or copse, as also probably 'beer' and 'bere' from Anglo-Saxon *beara*, a wood

bog – of the four Dartmoor terms for wet ground, bog and fen properly refer to the blanket bog, while mire and marsh are labels for basin and valley bogs

clapper bridge – granite slabs laid as imposts (spans) upon drystone piers

cleave – originally cliff, it has come to refer to the valley in which the cliff occurs

clitter – scatter of granite blocks on a hillside, the result of tor disintegration

coombe (combe) – valley

cut – moorman's name for an artificial pass through blanket bog

ford – ford does not necessarily refer to a river crossing; it can denote a way or track, or represent a variant of 'worthy' (see below)

gert – a cutting resulting from open-cast mining

growan – soft, coarse-grained, porous rock resulting from the decay of granite

hole – valley, but usually only part of it

in-country – the cultivated land abutting the moors

lake – always a stream on Dartmoor

leer – a locality selected and used by a moorman for depasturing livestock

logan rock – a rock which through weathering has become disjoined from the parent rock, being pivoted upon it

meet – confluence of steams

reave – originally simply a low bank, the term is now applied by archaeologists to the remains of prehistoric boundaries

rock basin – a natural rock hollow, often found on tors

swaling – controlled burning of moorland vegetation by commoners

tor – from the Celtic *twr*, this term has been regularized by geologists to refer to Dartmoor's distinctive outcrops of naked rock

well – spring

worthy – Old English derived suffix denoting a settlement or holding, of which 'ford', 'aford', 'over', 'aver', 'iver', 'ever', 'ary', 'ery' and 'eny' are variants. For example, Broadaford, in Widecombe parish, was recorded as Brodford in 1524, Bradworthy in 1634 and Broadover in 1843

Bibliography

British Geological Survey *British Regional Geology: South-West England* (4th edition), HMSO, London, 1975

Crossing, W *Guide to Dartmoor* (1912), David and Charles, Newton Abbot, reissued 1965 (ed. Brian le Messurier)

Gill C (ed.) *Dartmoor: a new study*, David and Charles, Newton Abbot, 1970

Greeves, T A P *Tin Mines and Miners of Dartmoor: A Pictorial Record*, Devon Books, Exeter, 1986

Harris, H *Industrial Archaeology of Dartmoor*, David and Charles, Newton Abbot, 1968

Harvey, L A and Gordon, D St Leger *Dartmoor*, Collins, London, 1953

Hemery, E *High Dartmoor: Land and People*, Robert Hale, London, 1984

Hoskins, W G *Devon* (1952), David and Charles, Newton Abbot, revised 1972

Rowe, S *A Perambulation of Dartmoor* (1848, revised 1896), Devon Books, Exeter, reissued 1985

Simmons I G (ed.) *Dartmoor Essays*, Devonshire Association for the Advancement of Science, Literature and Art, Devonshire Press, Torquay, 1964

Whitlock, R *The Folklore of Devon*, (1953 ed. G M Spooner and F S Russell) Batsford, London, 1977

Worth R H *Worth's Dartmoor*, David and Charles, Newton Abbot; reissued 1967

Useful addresses

Dartmoor National Park Authority
Parke
Haytor Road
Bovey Tracey
Devon TQ13 9JQ
(Tel: Bovey Tracey (0626) 832093)

Council for National Parks
45 Shelton Street
London WC2H 9HJ
(Tel: 01 240 3603)

Countryside Commission
South West Regional Office
Bridge House
Sion Place
Clifton Down
Bristol BS8 4AS
(Tel: Bristol (0272) 739966)

Dartmoor Preservation Association
Secretary
Crossings Cottage
Dousland
Yelverton
Plymouth
Devon

Devon Trust for Nature Conservation
35 New Bridge Street
Exeter
Devon EX4 3AH
(Tel: Exeter (0392) 79244)

National Trust
Devon Regional Office
Killerton House
Broadclyst
Exeter
Devon EX5 3LE
(Tel: Exeter (0392) 881691)

Nature Conservancy Council
Devon Office
49 Brook Street
Tavistock
Devon PL19 0BJ
(Tel: Tavistock (0822) 2292)

South West Water
Peninsula House
Rydon Lane
Exeter
Devon EX2 7HR
(Tel: Exeter (0392) 219666)

West Country Tourist Board
Trinity Court
Southernhay East
Exeter
Devon EX1 1QS
(Tel: Exeter (0392) 76351)

Further information

Weather: Local numbers for recorded forecasts based on Meteorological Office information: *Exeter* (0392) 8091; *Torquay* (0803) 8091; *Plymouth* (0752) 8091

Firing ranges: The Ministry of Defence has a large training area on the northern part of Dartmoor. Firing times are advertised in local newspapers every Friday and notices are displayed in local police stations, post offices and some inns; or use the telephone answering service on the following numbers: *Torquay* (0803) 24592; *Exeter* (0392) 70164; *Plymouth* (0752) 701924; *Okehampton* (0837) 2939

Index

Page numbers in *italics* refer to illustrations.